Praise for Jenna Bayley-Burke's
Private Scandal

"...as juicy as a soap opera and more fun than a day at the beach."

~ *Romantic Times Book Reviews*

"*Private Scandal* was a really enjoyable romance with lots of heartfelt emotion and some super hot love scenes. I highly recommend it."

~ *Romance Junkies*

Look for these titles by
Jenna Bayley-Burke

Now Available:

Her Cinderella Complex

Par for the Course

Compromising Positions

Pride and Passion

For Kicks

Private Scandal

Jenna Bayley-Burke

Love always wins!

SAMHAIN
PUBLISHING

Samhain Publishing, Ltd.
11821 Mason Montgomery Road, 4B
Cincinnati, OH 45249
www.samhainpublishing.com

Private Scandal
Copyright © 2012 by Jenna Bayley-Burke
Print ISBN: 978-1-60928-441-1
Digital ISBN: 978-1-60928-428-2

Editing by Heidi Moore
Cover by Scott Carpenter

First Samhain Publishing, Ltd. electronic publication: April 2011
First Samhain Publishing, Ltd. print publication: February 2012

Dedication

For Katie, who taught me how to have a best friend forever.

Chapter One

The façade of the coffee shop matched the other businesses in the strip mall—drab, dated and disappointing. Brandon Knight shook his head, knowing that the Pasadena planning commission's request to see the design plans for the new office park must be a mere formality. No one could possibly choose this over what the development company was offering to erect.

After this final meeting with the owner, all the obstacles would be cleared away. He was prepared to spend far more than the businesses were worth to make it happen. He made things happen.

They just weren't always the things he had planned.

He pulled opened the glass door and held it for a gaggle of teens hopped up on espresso. It gave him the chance to look inside at the dull hardwood floors, exposed pipes along the ceiling painted every neon color imaginable. Magazines, newspapers and board games littered the available tabletops. This place didn't just need a new location, it needed a complete makeover.

People seeking their mid-morning caffeine rush filled the tiny space. He slipped into line and a nervous sensation shimmied down his spine. No one seemed menacing or out of place, and yet he couldn't shake the unease. His gaze bounced from the mismatched chairs to the solid wood tables to the

Jenna Bayley-Burke

shelves of even more board games. His attention settled on the back of the barista. His gut twisted as his mind leapt with recognition.

Every time he saw natural blonde hair with more than a hint of curl, his heart vaulted. Even though this woman was too thin to be Megan, and dressed too plainly in dark jeans and a black T-shirt, his pulse raced in hopeful anticipation.

The line moved fast, the blonde barista making drinks and a goth brunette taking the orders. It was a well-oiled machine, and yet he couldn't help wishing he could catch the blonde's face so this misguided expectation would die already.

He ordered a grande Americano and stepped to the side to wait as she made his drink. Her hands were a flurry of motion as she made drinks two at a time. She was too busy to turn around, so he walked around the edge of the counter. She moved to the side to set two drinks down and nearly dropped them both.

Air sliced through his lungs as he caught her pale blue gaze. Her can-I-help-you smile curdled. Her name fell off his lips as he watched her expression amplify from shocked to furious in less than a second. He wanted to reach for her, to pull her into his arms and kiss her until they needed to come up for air.

She looked out into the café and called out the order, then turned back to the espresso machine and worked it with stunning ferocity.

"Megan," he called out again, trying to think over the pulse pounding in his brain. Megan was a socialite with a trust fund deep enough to buy and sell this place a hundred times over. Megan was supposed to be on a beach, sunning herself while her father avoided extradition for embezzlement. Megan couldn't be standing in front of him.

Yet here she was. A smaller, angrier version of the beautiful hotel heiress he loved.

He cleared his throat and tried to steady his swirling mind. "Megan, talk to me."

She flourished whipped cream atop two more drinks and then moved them to the counter without looking his way. It was almost as if she didn't recognize him.

"Meg, what are you doing here? Did you have some kind of accident?" His gut twisted at the idea that she had amnesia, that she might have been hurt and he hadn't been there to help her.

She said nothing, just pasted on a smile as she finished two more drinks and announced them to the people waiting.

"Megan," Brandon said again, trying to decide if he should leap over the counter.

"He ordered an Americano," the goth woman working the register said to Megan. "You skipped it."

"I'm not giving him a damned thing ever again." Megan worked the machine as she spoke, her expression hardening.

"He's a customer. Make his order, princess, or I get Lenny."

Brandon's eyes narrowed at the negative tone. Even with as angry as Megan was at him, he didn't have to watch someone talk down to her. "Megan, what are you doing here making coffee? What's going on?"

She said nothing, spared no extra movements as she worked the coffee grinder and espresso machine with an efficiency that impressed him. The clicks of the grinder, the whir of the steam, the slosh as she pumped syrup into the cups, all of it mixed together as he watched.

"Megan," he started, but didn't know what to say. He always knew what to say. "You owe me some kind of explanation."

"I owe you nothing." Megan spoke without looking at him. "You are a liar and a cheat and if I never see you again, it will be too soon."

"If this is about your father—"

"This is about you leaving me the hell alone. I don't know why you're here, and I don't care, as long as you leave." Her words were strong, but her hands were shaking, nearly spilling a macchiato.

"I'm not leaving."

"I'm getting Lenny." The brunette turned on her heel and marched through an archway into a back room.

Megan didn't miss a beat, finishing making orders and then taking the next one at the register. If he didn't know her so well he'd think she'd forgotten he was standing there, catching her in whatever game she was playing. He couldn't fathom what it could be.

He looked around the café for video cameras. Her sister had done a season of a celebutante reality show. Maybe Megan had gone that route too. He shook his head. Megan was intensely private.

After all, no one knew they'd been together for the last seven years.

"What seems to be the problem?" A dark-haired man emerged from the archway with the tattletale in tow. Brandon had come here to meet with Len Kulik, and the picture in the dossier was spot on for the young Russian immigrant looking to turn one coffee shop into a chain. Offering to invest in Kulik's dream would make the development deal smooth out considerably.

"Brandon Knight." He held out his hand and shook Len's,

smiling as recognition bloomed on the other man's face.

"I'm surprised you came yourself. Since your call I've been doing some research on your company."

"When something is important to me, I handle it personally." His gaze swept back to Megan as she shoved a handle on the espresso machine. She rolled her eyes at his words.

"Great, I'll be with you in just one minute." He turned to the goth chick. "I don't see any problem."

"The princess is refusing to serve him." She tilted her dark bob at Brandon.

"Megan," Len said. "Make his drink."

"No." Her voice was strong, but she clenched her jaw, which Brandon knew meant it was trembling. Megan was great at putting on a show and making the world think she had it all together even when things were falling apart.

The goth chick snorted and shook her head. "Told ya."

"Megan, your job is to make the drinks. Make his order." Lenny leaned closer to Megan than Brandon was comfortable with, but before he could object she spoke.

"Fine, I'll make it." She took her obvious hostility out on the machine as it perked and whooshed.

She was so angry that he wanted to tell her to forget the damned drink, forget the coffee shop, forget everything and just let him take her someplace where they could iron all this out.

He caught the wildness in her gaze as she turned to face him, the steaming drink in her hand. "I made your drink, but I won't let your lips near anything I've touched ever again." She let loose a string of expletives like he hadn't heard since military school, and none of them were the fun ones. He held up a hand to try and stop her from embarrassing herself further, but she ended the tirade.

Her last foul words still hung in the air when he saw the cup arc towards him. He jumped back, the cup connecting with his chest and spilling the scalding liquid down the front of his white dress shirt. If he hadn't arched his back, it would have really hurt.

"Megan!" Lenny cried out.

"Not to worry," Megan said as she marched towards the archway. "I quit."

Brandon Knight's sculpted physique blocked the stairs to her apartment as effectively as he'd barricaded her from the rest of her life.

And to think that she'd slept with him.

The southern California sun hadn't been out long enough to warm the early November day and the cool temperature crept through her thin coat. Her apartment within the walls of the aging cement and stucco building might not be much, but it was hers. She wanted to shove him aside, climb the stairs and lock him out as successfully as he'd locked her out of the only life she'd ever known. But she knew his body too well to think she might be able to move over six feet of muscle before he was good and ready. She leveled her gaze at him and cleared her throat, speaking over the whir of the traffic behind her.

"If you're thinking I'll invite you in for a cup of coffee, you've already had yours. Without my employee discount, I can't afford to douse you with another." Megan shifted her weight in her ankle boots, wishing she'd thought of a way to tell him off and still keep her job.

Brandon glanced down at the brown stain marring the

front of his perfect white shirt. *Not so perfect anymore.* She could only hope she'd ruined the suit as well.

"You could have burned me, Meg." His espresso-brown eyes were very serious, but his lips twitched, mocking her with a half smile.

"Considering how you've burned me, it would have been appropriate. Get out of my way, Brandon. Thanks to you I need to spend my day looking for a new job." Her weary body betrayed her at the words, her shoulders drooping in defeat. After working a closing shift at the bar last night and an early morning shift at the coffee house, she was running about two quarts low on sleep.

Unfortunately, she also needed to be able to make rent at the end of the month. As long as she could find something else quickly, the look on his face when she'd finally been able to tell him where to stick it would be worth the effort. Though for some ungodly reason, simply having him within slapping distance made her feel better, which was so counterproductive. She couldn't afford for him to make her stomach tumble, her knees weaken or any parts of her body warm. Not anymore.

She hitched her tangerine Prada satchel higher on her shoulder and shot him a look she hoped would kill him. Unfortunately, her efforts were as weak as her bank account. He didn't even move.

"We need to talk." He didn't move and her empty stomach began to knot. He really was cruel and heartless. Nothing but total desecration of her life would ever be enough for him.

"I can't think what about." She looked longingly up the cement stairs towards the dented metal door of her apartment. She'd thought it was safer to be on the second floor in this part of Pasadena, but she'd never considered Beverly Hills would decide to block her way.

"Let's start with earlier today."

"I'm sure it was a treat for you to watch me lose my job." Tension knotted between her shoulder blades.

"I seem to remember you quitting," he said, humor glinting in his eyes. "I know you're upset about what happened—"

"You don't know the first thing about me."

Somehow he closed the few steps between them in an instant, his fingers pressing into the flesh of her upper arm, his presence filling up her personal space. "I know everything about you, Megan. And if you don't want the world to know, I suggest we take this upstairs." He tilted his head towards one of the apartments beside the stairway. She didn't notice anything besides the planter box of dead plants and dingy welcome mat that had been there since she moved in last month.

She shrugged, more to get his hand off her than to give in to his demands. But with the movement, he stepped aside and she took the opportunity to climb the stairs, the heels of her boots clicking on every bare step.

"There isn't even a deadbolt?" he asked as she unlocked the door.

Megan didn't answer, just pushed the door open and was accosted by the stale smell and bare, yellow-tinged walls of the place she slept most afternoons, between being an early morning barista and late-night bartender. The inflatable mattress in the corner was covered with a faded quilt she'd smuggled out of her parents' house before the auctioneers had come to catalog everything. The hard-sided Louis Vuitton luggage did well enough as chairs, but she didn't want to invite him to sit.

"This is ridiculous, Megan." He punctuated the statement by slamming the door. "I don't know what you're trying to prove—"

"You're the one with something to prove. Was your daddy proud when you stole my family's company? Did he pat you on the head and tell you what a good corporate raider you'd become?" She laced her voice with saccharine, hoping the bitter undertone didn't shine through too brightly.

"I didn't steal a thing. That was your dad. I'm sorry if it hurts you, but—"

"Are you sorry?" She crossed her hands over her chest and wondered if it would matter.

"I'm sorry you're angry. But running away is a little adolescent."

"You can go now." She pulled the newspaper from her bag and set it on the chipped Formica countertop. For a fleeting moment she rued the loss of the dollar she'd had to pay for it, along with the jar of tips she'd forfeited by quitting. A few months ago she'd never thought about where her money went, and now the loss of less than fifty dollars had her near panic. She dropped her bag to the peeling linoleum floor and leaned against the bar as she batted open the pages until she found the employment section.

His hand came down on the paper with a slap. "If you don't want to explain what you're playing at, you can still listen to what I have to say."

Her shoulders tensed, but she refused to look up at him. Let him talk, let him leave. She needed him to go as much as she needed to find another job. Probably more. Because with him here, making the small room seem impossibly tiny with his larger-than-life presence, she had to think of just how far she'd fallen. She'd do anything not to have to analyze that. It was one of the reasons she needed to work so much. That, and she had an affinity for eating.

It was hard to imagine she used to think the perfect way to

end a night of clubbing with her so-called friends was to find her way to his penthouse. Harder still to imagine her life free of worry and fear.

Until she'd seen the look of shock and pity on Brandon's face, she'd been proud of all she'd accomplished. There was a satisfaction that came from independence and hard work that she'd never imagined. She'd come so far, and yet seeing Brandon reminded her of how far she'd fallen, how she might never get back to the safety and security she'd known.

The life of leisure and privilege was over, the last chapter a tragic ending written by Brandon when he'd taken Carlton Hotels from her family. Everything was auctioned and it still wasn't enough for the creditors. What more could Brandon want from her? Her very soul?

Megan wouldn't let him see her afraid. He'd caught her off-guard at the coffee shop, that was all. He'd stared at her across the counter with his bitter-chocolate eyes, derision in his voice when he asked what she was doing serving people coffee, and she'd snapped. She'd been reacting to him ever since.

Megan squared her shoulders and pulled in a deep breath. She was a Carlton, and though her father may have betrayed the responsibility of the name, she still believed in it. It was all she had left. Being a Carlton might not be worth much on the open market, but it meant she knew the best defense was a good offence. And she knew exactly how to play Brandon Knight.

After all, she'd been doing it for the better part of a decade.

She tossed her blonde hair over her shoulder and looked up at him, hoping her ice-blue eyes would work their magic. However, he seemed to be studying her like she'd grown an extra head. She started unbuttoning her coat, keeping her gaze on his face.

"You don't really want to talk, do you Brandon?"

He blinked as she slid the coat off her shoulders and set it on the counter. "I don't know where to begin."

"You, speechless? Never." She straightened her posture, grinning when the movement caused him to drop his gaze to the deep vee of her tight T-shirt. She'd learned quickly the more cleavage she showed, the more tips she'd find in the jar at the end of her shift.

"I want to know what you think you're doing. It's one thing to have a quarter-life crisis, but this is a bit extreme. I know what your father did was a shock—"

"It didn't surprise me half as much as you think. I knew he was a snake." She grinned, and he rewarded her efforts with a frown. Obviously he'd tired of her charms, but she'd known that, suffered that blow when she could least afford it.

"You knew he was embezzling from Carlton International?"

"I knew he was supporting more people than he could have on what he earned. Mistresses are quite expensive, as you know." Her throat tightened and she clenched her jaw to keep it from trembling.

"Then what are you doing? If you aren't upset about how he disappeared with millions of other people's money, why are you hiding out?"

"I'm not hiding."

"Megan, everyone thinks you're with your parents wherever it is they escaped to. And I find you making coffee and living like this?" He waved his hand through the air, forcing her to take another look at her sad apartment.

"Funny, isn't it? All those fundraisers I helped with for the Carlton Houses and they were full when I needed them." She shrugged. "It's amazing how few jobs there are for people who didn't bother to graduate high school."

"But you went to Beverly Prep." He rubbed at the back of his neck.

"And my mother needed an interpreter for her European vacation the spring of my senior year. I wasn't going to volunteer to go back." Megan pasted on her brightest smile. "It's fine. I got my GED last week. Maybe now I'll qualify to answer phones."

"But you speak three languages."

"So do the French and Germans. Now if I'd bothered to learn Spanish, I might have a bright future in telemarketing."

He ran his hand through his cropped dark brown hair. "That doesn't explain why you're here."

"Have you ever tried to get an apartment with no money, no job and no credit history? This was the best I could do."

"Please, Megan. Your trust fund—"

"Is probably what Daddy dearest is using to pay for his life on some island with no extradition agreement." The truth hung heavy between them. She hadn't meant to tell him, but she didn't have the energy to lie. She couldn't understand why her father would need to steal from his children if he'd taken all the money the newspapers claimed, but there were a lot of things about the situation she couldn't wrap her head around.

Brandon looked about the room. "Is this all you have?"

"I have what I need. Well, except for a day job."

He quirked a brow. "You have a night job?"

"The Blue Parrot. It's karaoke tonight. Will I see you there too?"

Brandon closed his eyes, his broad chest rising and falling with a deep breath. He opened his eyes, his dark gaze colliding with hers. "Get your things. You can stay with me."

"No, I can't." She'd rather die in Pasadena than have to listen to him having sex with Gemma Ryan down the hall. Besides, when she'd sold her things she'd vowed never to depend on anyone again.

"I can't let you stay here." The air in the small apartment sagged with tension.

"I don't see how what I do is any of your business." Part of her screamed to go with him, to find a safe and clean place where she wouldn't be scared and lonely. She wanted so desperately to escape what her life had become, but at least now it was of her own making.

"It's ridiculous for you to be here."

"No, it's ridiculous for *you* to be here, pretending that it matters to you. You got what you wanted from the Carltons. You'll excuse me if I don't offer my congratulations on your accomplishments."

He crossed his arms over his chest. "Do you need help packing?"

And to think she used to find his confidence attractive. Hell, she still did. "I'm not going anywhere with you. I'm never sleeping with you again. You can take that to the bank. It's much more secure than any investment you've ever made."

"Did I ask you?" His gaze bore holes in what was left of her bravado. "If you don't want to come home with me, I'll put you up in a hotel until we figure this out. If you want a job, I'm sure I can find something that makes better use of your talents."

If his gaze hadn't slid down her body at the words, she might have believed his altruistic intentions. But she knew Brandon, knew his insatiable desires better than anyone. She'd relished it when it was on her terms, but to be beholden to him? Being with him lost all appeal in the light of what he'd done, who he'd turned her into. Not to mention the piece of trash

21

currently keeping his sheets warm.

"I'm not sleeping with you, not living with you, not working for you. In fact, I'd prefer not to breathe the same air. With you around everything has the stink of betrayal."

"This is how you want it?"

Not at all, but she didn't see any other option. She nodded.

He stepped closer, until she couldn't move without touching him. "Be careful what you wish for."

His words echoed back in time, the scene unfolding in her mind of when he'd said that to her all those years ago. She'd flirted with him shamelessly. He was everything she'd thought she wanted, even though she knew he was more than she could handle. He'd refused her every advance, until she returned from Europe. She couldn't hide the shiver that ran down her spine at the memory.

Brandon lifted her chin with his fingers and brushed his lips across hers. Megan froze, her heart pounding a primal beat in her chest. A surge of heat coursed through her body and she pulled in a breath to cool the desire. It didn't work. It never did. Somehow, through the hazy memory of all she'd lost, she pulled away.

She gazed up at him, wishing she could hate him. "I slept with you because you were my friend. You most certainly are not my friend, so you aren't entitled to those kinds of benefits anymore."

"For the record, Meg, I have wanted more from you for a while now. I'm done sneaking around and playing games. Next time you're in my bed—and believe me, there will be a next time—you won't be leaving."

Brandon stopped dead at the bottom of the stairs. A bus,

like the one Megan had arrived home on moments before, rumbled past. When it was gone he saw the stark difference in the way he and Megan now travelled.

His vintage Corvette, her city bus.

How had he let this happen? He'd been so sure the Carlton deal would tilt everything in his favor, but somehow it threw his plans wildly off track. For a man unaccustomed to making mistakes, it really set him off balance.

He sat down on the cold steps and pulled out his phone, speed dial connecting him almost immediately.

"Was she there?" Humor laced Danny Reid's voice.

"That she was. You any closer to figuring out why?" Computer keys clicked in the background. It seemed Danny's knack for uncovering corporate secrets played well in the personal realm. What hadn't they taught the man in Special Ops?

"She's been in Pasadena for months. When the receiver stepped in to liquidate the assets Carlton left, Megan went to a hotel with her sisters. They stayed until the hotel management realized their credit cards had been frozen. They left, but the bill wasn't paid until last month, in cash. They all kept things pretty quiet."

"Which is why everyone assumes they joined their parents." He plucked at the stain on the front of his shirt. Why hadn't she come straight to him?

She'd been finding her way to him for longer than he cared to think about. No one knew about it. She'd been adamant about that. It was a fun arrangement when he was younger, but when he turned thirty last year he'd told her he needed more. She'd been steadily ignoring that fact ever since, though she did accept the key card to his penthouse, still had plenty of clothes there. If he hadn't been so busy, he would have pushed the issue and they would have been married before the Carlton deal went public.

"Megan and Briana haven't been in contact with anyone. Most people know Ava is shacked-up with Sullivan, the computer genius with that IPO you made a mint on?"

"I know who he is." Brandon wondered why Ava had let her sister live in a place like this if she was with Jack Sullivan. Every time he found a missing piece, he realized the puzzle was bigger than he expected. "And Briana?"

"She's in Oregon living with an aunt and interning at a hotel up there. Megan is the one hiding. If she wasn't in on it, she's sure acting like she has something to hide."

Yeah, like embarrassment. If Carlton had cashed in one trust fund, he likely liquidated them all.

None of it explained why Megan was so hell bent on not accepting help from anyone. He begrudged the admiration he felt for how she'd picked herself up. She was being stubborn to the point of ridiculous, but a part of him understood. Even if his bank account flatlined, he'd have options an education and experience provided.

Why hadn't he realized she never graduated? His chest tightened. Because he'd been too damned excited when she'd returned from Europe to have realized there was no graduation party.

Brandon tugged on his earlobe and straightened his posture. The past didn't matter. He needed to focus on keeping Megan safe.

Across the street a pair of unruly looking teens made their second pass past his Corvette. His gut knotted. He could buy a dozen sports cars, but if anything happened to Megan he'd never forgive himself.

"Danny, Megan's not hiding anything." It wouldn't fit in the room she called an apartment.

"She's paying cash for everything. Nothing is traceable. If she's not hiding, why else would she go off the grid?"

He opened his mouth to explain exactly how he knew Megan wouldn't be here if she had any other options, but he couldn't. His knowledge of her affinity for expensive sheets and sleeping late wasn't public. More than that, he knew her, knew her rigid sense of fairness that extended from domestic abuse to equal time with the remote control. He knew by looking into her eyes that this wasn't the childish snit he'd first thought, but a true act of bleak desperation.

What he didn't know was why.

Following her home before he had all the facts wasn't his smartest move, and neither was sitting on her stairway, wondering how someone so vibrant and alluring could be in a place so dull and depressing. He'd built his success by knowing more than his competition, by paying attention to details others overlooked. And yet where Megan was concerned, he'd always been blind.

In the last seven years he's spent more nights with her than without. It had been an absolutely ideal situation, one most of his friends would trade anything for. A beautiful, intelligent woman in his private life who wanted nothing to do with the public trappings of his work. He hadn't realized just how good he'd had it until Megan disappeared.

Danny's laugh broke into his thoughts. "Okay, so you obviously have no idea what her motivation is. But this isn't your problem, man. She's Carlton's daughter, not yours. And while she might have chosen the seedier side of Pasadena, she has a job and a place to stay and an obvious dislike of you. So why don't you get off the guilt train and get back to work?"

His chest grew tight at the truth of his friend's words.

Megan was all kinds of angry and not in any mood to change her disposition. "I need you to run a check on her financials, hers and her sisters. The girls' trust funds weren't accessible in the receivership, but she's claiming her father tapped them before he disappeared."

"And you're actually buying that? He took the liquid assets of the corporation because he knew you were bearing down on him."

"We have no idea what Carlton was thinking before he split, or if Megan had any role in it. And I need some kind of bodyguard on her. Something."

"Why? Do you think she's in communication with her father? Maybe she can lead us to him and the money he stole from the company." Computer keys clicked in the background while Danny undoubtedly set the world in order.

"I want whoever is watching her to be someone who'll intercede if necessary. She can't get hurt in this, Danny." Not more than she already had.

"You need to come back to work and get your mind off Carlton's girls. You can't save the world. Believe me, I've tried."

"Not the world, just her." Brandon rose from the steps and walked to his car with icy determination. It hadn't been luck, but planning, instinct and perseverance that earned him the success he now enjoyed.

He needed to approach the Megan situation the way he did a business deal. Information first, action next. The next time he saw Megan Carlton, he'd be prepared.

She'd be the one reeling.

Chapter Two

In the late-morning lull, Megan emptied out the tip jar and headed to the back office of the coffee shop to divide the tips. She wasn't sure why they'd hired her back when she'd come in to apologize after realizing all the crap jobs in Pasadena were taken. However, she didn't really care so long as she earned enough money to pay off her exorbitant cell-phone bill and buy a new charger. Her life was on that phone and since the battery died she'd had no way to contact anyone.

She'd skated through the first twenty-five years of her life without a plan, and that blew up in her face in spectacular fashion. Once she got everything back in order, no one and nothing would throw her into such disarray ever again. Brandon hadn't bothered her again in the last week, cementing the realization that she'd been terribly wrong about trusting him in the first place.

She sorted the money into two piles, one for her and one for Wendy, who'd worked the shift with her. As the money added up, she did a mental calculation of what she'd saved and realized she'd be able to pay off what she owed on the phone today, maybe even sweet talk the guy at the store into ordering the charger since she should have enough for it by the time it arrived. Hopefully it was a guy at the store. The last two times she'd been in, the women had been less than helpful, not even letting her charge the phone for a few minutes so she could copy some numbers off.

"I don't think it's fair for us to split the money."

"Really?" Megan looked up to where Wendy stood in the doorway to the small office. Wendy had spent most of the morning sitting at a table with one of her friends instead of helping customers, but she usually did that.

"This is some kind of reality show thing for you, right? I've seen you and your celebrity friends on television." She flicked her black hair off her face, the sleeve of her shirt inching higher with the move and revealing a purple bruise.

Megan's stomach lurched and knotted. "Do you see cameras anywhere?"

"They must be hidden. I figure it's some kind of experiment that you'll get to laugh about next year when it's in prime time. I shouldn't have to split tips with you. It's not fair."

"That bruise on your arm doesn't look fair." She met the woman's gaze, recognizing the shame as Wendy tugged down her sleeve.

"You don't know what you're talking about. I hit my arm on a door."

"I know people you can talk to. They know how to help you, keep you safe." Megan glanced down at the money, wishing she didn't need it.

"I don't want to be part of your TV crusade. Keep me out of your reality show, okay? I know how they work. You do this crazy thing and bored people get to watch, and the next thing you know, you're famous for no reason. I'll still be right here, and I shouldn't have to share money with you. I have real problems, bigger than which dress to wear on the red carpet."

Megan stacked the bills in two piles, placing the change on

top. "Maybe you don't make it past the entertainment section of the newspaper, but my father nearly bankrupted a company. I'm working here because I need to, not for publicity." She grabbed her bag and pulled out one of the white cards she kept in the inside pocket. "If you need the money today, you can have it. But I won't do it again unless you call this number." She slid the two piles of money together and placed the card on top.

Wendy lifted the card and read. "Evelyn Hattem Catering?"

"If he finds it, tell him she offered you a waitressing job at parties she caters." Megan stood, pulling her bag onto her shoulder.

"You don't understand."

"You're right. I don't understand why women don't leave the first time it happens. It doesn't just stop."

"I have a kid and two dogs. It's not that easy to just walk away. You don't get to judge me."

"I'm not." Her heart tugged at the realization that animals often kept people in bad situations. Before her life went to hell in a handbasket, she'd been trying to work out a way for the Carlton Houses to accept animals as well. "If you need my share of the tips, you're welcome to them. If it's for him, I have better things to spend my money on."

Wendy nodded and grabbed both stacks of cash. "I'll think about calling."

"Don't ask for my tips again until you have. You can count out the till. I'm out of here."

Megan made her way out of the coffee shop, the bell on the door ringing her departure. After six hours on her feet last night and six again this morning with only an hour in between, she should go home and sleep before she started the whole cycle over again. But she knew she wouldn't be able to sleep, not now.

As the day crept towards noon, the air warmed around her while she walked the mile and a half to the reason she'd landed in Pasadena. Her mother had funded the first Cassie Carlton Retreat House twenty years ago to honor Megan's great-grandmother and the founder of the Carlton Hotel empire. Even with the loss of its major benefactor, the charity was still running.

For now.

Megan stopped at the white picket fence, looking up at the non-descript façade. To those who passed by, it was just another home in an old neighborhood. For her, it was a sanctuary whose walls had saved countless women. It was the embodiment of what her great-grandmother stood for, of how far she came from a battered wife to boarding house manager to hotelier. She'd made a plan for how her life would be and nothing got in her way.

With new determination, Megan made her way down the front path and around to the back door where she used the numbered lock to let herself in.

"Megan? I'm surprised to see you," Evie said, piling up the paperwork she'd been busy with. The home's director often worked at the kitchen table so she'd be open to any of the guests who might need to talk. "I thought you were working today."

"I'm done for a few hours, so I thought I'd check in." She sunk into one of the chairs and listened to the quiet of the house. "The kids left?"

Evie nodded and shrugged. "They packed up most everything this morning and headed to a cousin's house in Oregon."

"Briana went to Oregon. I don't suppose she's called?" She

missed her sisters terribly. One of the reasons she was so focused on the cell phone was to be able to use the numbers in it to track them down.

She'd almost given in last week and asked Brandon if he'd tracked down her sisters the way he had her. Was he simply after the money her father had embezzled and not above using the man's children to find it, or did seven years of sharing her body with him mean he owed her the thinnest sliver of responsibility?

Not enough to warn her that her life was about to implode, or even keep other women out of his bed. Her heart and eyes began to ache, so she put the image of Brandon and Gemma Ryan firmly out of her mind.

Evie shook her head. "A fresh start will do them all good, I think. And it means we have a room, if you still need it."

"Actually, that's why I'm here. There's a woman from work who might be calling."

"Are you sure you won't marry me?" Gemma Ryan all but stomped into Brandon's office and perched on his leather couch, her pout in full force. "It's just a year of your life. What do you have to do this year that you can't do married to me?"

Brandon watched from behind the open armoire as Danny turned his wheelchair around behind the large mahogany desk. His smile was as big as her eyes.

"If you have your heart set on getting married today, sweetheart, we can leave right now." Danny leaned on his elbow, tilting his body towards the pretty blonde.

When Gemma jumped in shock, Brandon couldn't help but laugh. He supposed sitting down and from behind he and

Danny looked enough alike—short dark hair, broad shoulders, the obligatory dress shirt and tie. But the wheelchair wasn't the only way to tell them apart. Dan shaved twice a day, while Brandon put it off until he couldn't pass it off as stylish shadow anymore.

"This isn't funny." Gemma turned to look at Brandon, then gestured towards Danny. "Did you tell him?"

After collecting the paper he needed, Brandon closed the armoire and walked to his desk. "This is your train wreck, not mine. Though you should tell him. He knows everything about everyone. He could tell you who's likely to milk you for your inheritance faster than I could."

"Wow, Gemma, train wrecks, marriage and an inheritance? You're a movie of the week, darlin'." Danny wheeled around to the front of the desk.

"I told you, this isn't funny."

"No, you told him it wasn't funny, me you tend to ignore. But if you want to look my way, we can head to the courthouse right now."

"I can't marry you."

"Of course you can't, honey." Dan leaned back in the chair and patted the padded armrests.

"That's not why!"

Brandon cleared his throat. "You know, Gem, he's not a bad option. I trust him with my life."

"Really." Gemma leveled her gaze at him, and then turned to Danny. "Do you know who he's marrying?"

Danny's head whipped around. "What is with the matrimonial fever in this room?"

"He claims he can't marry me because he is marrying someone else, but he won't tell me who."

Suspicion flickered in Danny's gaze before he turned back to Gemma. "He's no prince charming, sweetheart. I'm definitely a better catch."

"Would you be serious!"

"Why do you want to marry him anyway? He works too much, his feet stink and he snores."

"Hey! Those were your shoes you were always smelling, and I do not snore." The trouble with staying friends with someone who had watched you go through the most awkward and malodorous years of adolescence was that no matter how you grew up, you were still that angry kid who got tossed into military school for having one too many parties at his parents' house. Actually, it was the party on the yacht that sent him to Colvard Military Institute. He had to grin at all he learned there. It was as much about how to behave as it was about how to not get caught misbehaving.

"Don't listen to him. He snores like a bear."

"No, I don't." Megan had never said anything, and she wasn't the type to keep something like that to herself. Though she never slept over as often as he liked, but he always thought that had more to do with her need for privacy than him.

"Go on then," Danny motioned for the phone. "Let's call your bride and ask."

Brandon only glared. He'd figured Danny had begun to put things together about Megan, but this confirmed it.

"I knew you weren't really getting married." Gemma sat up straighter.

"No, he is. Well, he wants to, his bride isn't as convinced he's husband material as you are."

She slumped back into the cushions and looked at Brandon. "What about Dane Preston? Do you—"

"Gay," Danny said.

"Excuse me?" Gemma's long hair cascaded over her shoulder as she tilted her head to the side.

"He's gay."

Brandon drummed his fingers on his desktop. "For her purposes, that wouldn't matter. But he's too much of a risk."

"The gambling thing?" Danny looked up at him. Brandon nodded in response. Danny shook his head and wheeled closer to where Gemma sat. "Okay, so let me get this straight, princess. You're okay with marrying a gay guy or a guy who's hopelessly hung up on someone else, but the string of pretty boys you play with aren't in the line-up. Why is this?"

Gemma shot him a desperate look, but Brandon could only shrug. "Go ahead, tell him."

She narrowed her gaze and then turned to Danny. "My grandfather decided to make my inheritance contingent upon being married for one year by my thirtieth birthday. I have a month to get married, or else next year my inheritance will go to some Antarctic exploration fund."

"Ah, the last frontier."

"This isn't a joke."

"You don't want to get married, then get a job, princess. It's not as if you didn't know this was coming. It sounds to me like you've known for a while you'd have to hitch up."

"It's not just about the money. It includes the Ryan Estate. All those people would have to find new homes because I doubt some Antarctic explorer is going to want to hold on to an Alzheimer's center." Her face reddened and her voice rose with each word. She swallowed hard and seemed to gain her control back. "I can't marry just anyone off the street. There's a clause that I can't have a prenuptial agreement. It has to be someone I trust not to stick with me for a year and then rob me blind in the divorce. It isn't worth doing if I'm going to lose everything anyway."

Brandon scratched his head and shifted in his seat. "It's not that I don't want to help you, Gemma. But I can't marry you."

"Because of this mystery woman. Are you sure she's worth me losing everything?" There was desperation in her dark green gaze, but it didn't tempt him in the slightest. Neither had the kiss she's planted on him a few months back when she first told him about her crazy scheme. He wanted Megan and nothing was ever going to change that.

A smile slowly spread across his face. Megan was worth any risk. But he didn't have to throw his friends to the wolves either, just at each other. "Danny and I will think on it for you. There's got to be a man in California who doesn't need to marry you for your money."

"I guess if that's the best you're going to offer, there's nothing more I can do." Gemma rose, brushing a hand over the imaginary wrinkles in her skirt. He got up from the desk and circled around to hug her before she left. She was so defeated by all this that he knew he had to think of some way out of it for her.

Once she was gone, he sat on the edge of his desk and waited. Danny kept quiet for long minutes before speaking.

"You're really going to marry Megan Carlton?"

"First chance I get."

By the time she got off the second bus, Megan realized she really should have slept for more than an hour yesterday. Even though it was mid-day, it wasn't safe to be nodding off on public transportation, especially with a transient eyeing your handbag.

Luckily, the sun on her face bolstered her enough to fake alertness as she walked to her apartment. In the last two weeks she'd been working both jobs every day, volunteering at Carlton House, and barely sleeping more than an hour at a time. It seemed every time she'd drift off, she'd hear something that spooked her—cars backfiring, neighbors fighting, kids playing a joke and trying to open her front door. At least she hoped it was a joke. Either way, she couldn't relax and was running on nothing but adrenaline and caffeine.

It felt like treading water in the middle of a deserted ocean, no rescue in sight. Wendy had been talking with Evelyn, and collecting double tips for it. Megan wanted to help, but she couldn't afford to for much longer. Each month that she didn't pay off her old cell-phone bill, they tacked on a ridiculous interest fee. It was as if they expected her to dig her way to China with a runcible spoon. She'd even started going to other electronics stores looking for the charger, but it seemed her phone wasn't a standard model. Of course. Ava had picked them out, and she always got the latest thing.

Megan walked faster, hoping momentum would carry her far enough to get behind a locked door before she crashed. She was so exhausted even her brain was tired, so she might actually get some sleep rather than lying awake and wondering about her family.

"Where have you been?" The deep voice rocked her back on her heels and the slamming of a car door sent adrenaline rushing through her veins. She grabbed for the can of pepper spray on her keys as her brain slowly registered the hulking figure walking towards her.

She had half a mind to spritz him with the pepper spray

anyway. "Damn it, Brandon. You scared me."

"I shouldn't have. I've been watching you for two blocks. If you're going to live in a place like this, you need to be aware of your surroundings." He crossed his arms over his chest, his shirt bunching around his shoulders with the movement.

"You shouldn't jump out in front of women, or you might find yourself on the wrong end of a can of mace. There, we're even. One piece of advice for another." She stepped off the curb, hoping to get across the street and up the stairs before Brandon caught up with her.

His fingers wrapped around her arm, keeping her from fleeing. "I saw Ava."

Megan froze. The problem with sleeping with the enemy was that they knew exactly where you were vulnerable. She needed to know that her sisters were all right. She hadn't spoken with either of them since they were thrown out of the hotel and Briana decided to visit the cat-loving aunt they hadn't seen in twenty years.

They used to talk almost every hour, and now the only sound between them was silence. She needed to hear their voices, but she'd settle for knowing one of them was okay.

She turned to face Brandon, cocking her head to the side and trying to appear haughty for all she was worth, which wasn't much anymore. "And?"

"She said you had quite the fight, you know, about me. It seems that to her, you were all about defending my honor. And yet when I see you, you can't be bothered to even step on my toes. What's that about, Meg?"

"I didn't have all the facts. It turned out you are every bit as cold and ruthless as my sister thought."

"Come on now, Meg. Cold isn't something I've ever been around you."

"You don't feel the chill?" She stared into his dark eyes, wishing she'd realized that what she'd read as concern for all those years hadn't been anything close.

He met her gaze and held it, doing the most convincing acting job of appearing hurt. As if she could do him any damage. Nothing another big deal and Gemma Ryan couldn't soothe, anyway. She shook off his arm and took a step back.

"What else did Ava say?"

"You want to know, get in the car." He used the remote to unlock the doors on his Escalade.

"I'm not going anywhere with you."

"I'm not discussing your sister in the middle of the street. So either you get in the car and let me take you to lunch like the civilized woman you used to be, or we go upstairs to what you call an apartment and talk through what is going on. Your choice." He opened the passenger door of the SUV and stood beside it.

If he needed to tell her something about Ava in private, it couldn't be good. Her gut twisted with fear and the memory of the last time she'd seen her older sister. They'd fought horribly about where to go and what to do. Ava had always let men use her, sleeping with guys who didn't deserve her time, let alone her body. And she'd thought that was the solution again, find a boyfriend who'd let them move in until everything was sorted out. It was sad, more so because Megan had left the hotel with the intention of asking Brandon for help, and found his lips occupied by a tramp he'd always described as a *friend*.

She shook her head, refusing to wallow in her own mistakes. If Ava was in trouble, she needed to know about it. Better to find out the details in public. Whenever Brandon was too close, she tended to forget about what she'd seen in that hallway.

Not wanting to give Brandon the satisfaction of hearing her agree to his demands, she merely climbed into the passenger seat and buckled herself in while he closed the door. The smell of his aftershave swirled around her, but she refused to let it remind her of what used to be. He was Gemma's now. Maybe she ought to find a way to let the tramp know just who'd picked out this particular scent for him.

She stared out the window as Brandon got in and started the SUV. She'd always been careful to keep things private, to maintain a clandestine air about their relationship. It was supposed to keep things exciting, keep him from getting bored and moving on. Her father had once said the surest way to get a man to leave was to ask him to stay, so she never gave herself the option. She'd always been the one to leave, showing up unexpectedly to keep him off-balance.

When Brandon started hinting about making their relationship more public, Megan had been purposely aloof. He'd said he wanted a ring on her finger, but he never bought one. He'd claimed he wanted to be able to take her out, but he never invited her. It had given her a hope that she knew better than to have.

Men like him, men like her father, didn't love anything but the thrill of the chase—whether they were chasing women or money. She'd thought she could outplay him, but he moved faster than the scenery outside the car window. She closed her eyes and prayed Ava hadn't been burned the same way.

"Are you asleep?"

Megan blinked at the sound of Brandon's voice, unsure if she had drifted off. "Of course not."

Yet somehow the car had stopped at an Italian chain restaurant they often had delivered. As she blinked to awareness, she realized this would be the first time they went to a restaurant together. Sure, they'd shared a meal alongside dozens of their common friends at parties, but whenever they were alone, they were always ensconced in his penthouse. It was right across from her father's, so no one ever questioned her coming and goings from the hotel. She'd thought she was being so smart, but in the end she'd learned the hard way what a fool she'd been.

Glancing over at him was a mistake. The look in his warm brown eyes could easily be mistaken for kindness, she could simply ignore that it must be pity. Guilt might be niggling at his conscience and she wondered if Gemma Ryan knew him well enough to notice.

It wasn't that he was with Gemma that ripped at Megan's heart—she knew men would never be faithful for long—but she did wonder how long he'd managed to juggle them both. She'd never seen it coming, never felt any of the twinges of suspicion that women talked about. Maybe because she'd never had a right to, maybe because she had a knack for showing up in his bed unannounced and uninvited, and he'd always been alone.

"Are you hungry?" Brandon asked, the pity evident in his weak smile.

"Not in the slightest," she lied, clutching her bag to her middle. She was painfully close to having enough cash for the phone charger, and she wasn't about to waste her money on food. She could eat again at work, except she didn't work either job until Wednesday, two days away. Still, lunch here would use up a quarter of what she'd managed to save since she'd forfeited her tips to Wendy.

His gaze swept her body. "You're too thin. Doesn't that scare you?"

While he climbed out of the car and circled around to open her door, Megan glanced down at herself as if for the first time.

She'd always been the thicker Carlton sister, but it wasn't much of a club. Ava had curves that left too many men drooling, while Megan had a chocolate addiction, or had when she'd been able to afford it.

She slipped out of the car, her mind still reeling with the realization her skinny jeans were being held up by a belt, while Brandon's hand at the small of her back steered her into the restaurant and to their table.

The heavenly aromas of garlic and herbs danced around her as she tried to focus on the bowl of ramen noodles she'd make when she got home. When the waitress arrived with a basket of warm breadsticks, Megan's hand twitched under the table. She swallowed hard and her stomach grumbled in protest.

Brandon stared at her, as if daring her to give in and order, but she merely shook her head and dug her fingernails into her palms. She was here to find out what he knew about Ava. After that, she'd figure out just where they were and take a bus back to the apartment. This wasn't a date. It was his guilt dragging him down to slum with her.

He shook his head and flashed a megawatt smile at the waitress. "She'll have a diet cola and the mixed grill, hold the potatoes. I'll get the seafood alfredo and iced tea."

"Water is fine for me, actually." She wasn't about to take in any more caffeine. When she made it back to her mattress, she had a date with as much sleep as she could manage. Megan hoped her Hollywood smile matched his. Either way, the waitress didn't seem to notice their display at all before she bustled away.

"You need to eat, Megan."

"What I do is none of your business. I came here so you would tell me about my sister."

He stared at her as if she'd started speaking a foreign language. She met his gaze and held it, loathing each time she had to blink.

"No." Brandon reached into the basket and took out a breadstick. Steam wafted up as he broke it in half.

"Then I'm leaving." She scooted her chair out and wished she'd paid attention during the drive. There was no telling where they were or how many busses she'd have to take to get back to her illustrious Pasadena abode.

"I'll tell you everything I know if you'll eat something. You're scaring me, Megan. For the first time in forever I don't know what is going on with you and you've completely shut me out."

The man should be an actor. He had the looks for it and managed to deliver that little spiel with enough conviction to convince anyone he cared. Anyone who hadn't had him steal her family fortune and cheat on her on the same day. There really wasn't any coming back from that.

She settled into her chair and slid her bag to the ground. If he was feeling so guilty about just how far she'd fallen, then maybe he should buy her lunch. Maybe a glass of wine and dessert too. She hadn't wasted money on either in far too long and he owed her in spades.

Brandon Knight had dragged her here under the pretense of telling her about her sister, the least he could do was pay for a meal. That's what Ava would say anyway. Happy with her new decision, Megan reached for a breadstick of her own.

"So Brandon, what's new with you? Any other lives you've scuttled lately?" She bit into the soft breadstick, the warmth intensifying the garlic flavor.

"Megan." He cleared his throat and wiped his hands on his napkin. "I did not steal your family's company. I saved it. Your dad—"

"You say potato..." She rolled her eyes. "You're a corporate raider. It's what you do. It's not personal, it's business. Pardon me if I happen to find what went down very personal."

"I am an activist shareholder. He was bleeding the entire corporation. If I hadn't managed to get him out of control and have the board sell off the subsidiaries, your precious Carlton Hotels would have been bankrupt."

"It's yours now. There's not a Carlton in the mix anymore." She leaned back in her chair and wished the waitress would return so she could order wine, maybe a whole bottle.

"Did you ever stop and think I bought it because I knew what it meant to you? You want so badly to paint me the villain in this, but I didn't do anything wrong."

She froze, anger boiling up from deep within her. It took her a few breaths before she could speak without wanting to spear him with a fork. Lucky for her, she'd had months to think about what she'd say to him.

"Spare me your guilt-induced back pedaling. If you don't like yourself very much right now, it's because of what you did, not how I reacted to it. It's one thing to play me as hard and as rough as you did, it's quite another to try and wrap it up in a pretty package and call it altruistic. Millionaires quake when you start buying into their companies because they know you plan on restructuring them right out of their income bracket, not because you are known for being soft and cuddly."

"I'm talking about this deal, Meg." He tapped his finger on the table for emphasis. "This deal, not all the ones I did before or have done since. He was destroying something you were proud of."

"I'm sorry, but my father isn't at this table. I'm talking about you, Brandon Knight. If you really were trying to save Carlton Hotels for me, you would have told me before it all went down."

"If I would have told you, you would have run straight to him."

"You do see where your selfless logic gets fuzzy here, right?"

Brandon's chest rose and fell as he huffed a deep breath. "You are exasperating. How hard is it to see that I was trying to do this for you, as a gift."

"La Perla is a gift, Brandon." She tamped down the images of just how much of the pricey lingerie he'd given her over the years. "Taking my family's business for your own isn't something you do to say happy birthday."

He had the decency to look apologetic. "The timing stunk, but it couldn't be helped."

"I don't care about your flimsy explanations. Let Carlton Hotels be a souvenir of a relationship gone wrong and leave me alone."

He leaned back in his chair and stared at her over steepled fingers. "No."

Chapter Three

"What do you mean no?"

"It's a simple word, Meg. I know you weren't accustomed to it, especially from me, but I am not going to just walk away and leave you to whatever this destructive game is that you're playing with your life."

"See, right there, it's my life."

The waitress arrived with two steaming plates of food just as Megan was looking about the table for cutlery to filet him with. He was the most infuriating man. As the waitress moved to set Brandon's plate of pasta in front of him, Megan grinned and reached out.

"Actually, that's for me." Without batting a false eyelash, the waitress set the cream laden pasta in front of Megan, serving Brandon the grilled meat and vegetables. How he hated vegetables.

Megan quickly twirled her fork into the fettuccini, feeling better than she had all day. In her previous life, she'd been too concerned about calories and carbs to indulge in something so decadent. Let Brandon be good with the zucchini and peppers, she was going to comfort herself with scallops and parmesan.

"Could you bring a bottle of sauvignon blanc?" She named her favorite Napa valley vintage and only wondered for two seconds about the price. "One glass. He's driving."

"Sure thing." The waitress was only gone long enough for Megan to get through her first bite before returning with the wine. Megan swirled the wine in her glass and breathed in the fresh scent of passion fruit and lime. One sip and she reveled in the zesty citrus taste. She loved how wine could encompass so many flavors at once.

"That wine goes with your lunch." Brandon gave the hills of pasta a hungry glance.

"It really does." Megan smiled and took another sip, glad Brandon got to be the one to want something he couldn't have for once. "Are you going to tell me what you know about my sister now?"

He used his fork to play with the vegetables, and then seemed to give up and lay it aside. "Ava is in New York."

Megan blinked slowly. "You're kidding."

"She's starting her own business."

Maybe there was something to Wendy's reality-television theory. Megan looked around for cameras, because the only thing Ava was driven to do was the chauffer.

"It seems like she and Sullivan are pretty serious."

"Sullivan?"

"Jack Sullivan? Quiet guy, designed those computer games for that social networking site and made a mint."

Megan pulled her shoulders back and wondered what kind of alternative universe her sister had walked into, and where she might find the door. "She stopped going out with him because he never tried to sleep with her, and you know how every guy wants to get with Ava. She thought he was using her as some kind of beard."

"He's a pretty stand-up guy. She looks as if what went down is the best thing that ever happened to her. Well, except she's worried about you since you haven't returned her calls or emails."

Megan closed her eyes and shook her head, wishing she'd been able to get the phone working by now. Ava seemed to have taken her idea to find a guy willing to support her until she was back on her feet all the way to the bank. But more than that, if what Brandon was saying were true, Ava might just have grown up, at least a little. She looked over at Brandon and a wave of sadness washed over her again. When she needed him most, he'd been face-first in another woman. She prayed Jack Sullivan really did ride in on a white horse.

"Your sister is worried about the fight you two had the last time she saw you."

"Did you tell her that I'm fine and how to find me?"

"You haven't been taking her calls or emails, so I assumed you didn't want her to know about your current...situation."

"I don't have an email address except the one I use for fundraising for the shelter. She hasn't sent anything there. Maybe she signed me up for one to go along with that ridiculously expensive phone she gave me. It's been dead since before we fought, and a new charger costs more than I've been able to pull together."

"A cell-phone charger is like twenty bucks. I have a drawer full of them."

Megan shook her head. "Ava had to have these phones that charge using a power pad. There is nowhere to plug anything into the phone, so they look sleek, but unless you have your little power phone mat, you're sunk."

"She bought one of those?"

"She bought three. She's always looking to get the next thing before everyone else." Megan tucked into the pasta again. "What kind of business is she starting?"

"Some online thing renting purses. It doesn't make much sense to me but she's excited about it and Sullivan thinks it will float. She's already done a test market."

The food and wine weren't helping. She was supposed to be the savvy Carlton sister. Ava was sexy, Briana was smart, and yet the *savvy* one had a GED and an apartment on the wrong side of Pasadena. Somewhere along the way she'd miscalculated and her high road had taken her very low.

Brandon continued to pepper the silence with random bits about her sisters' new lives. Briana's classes at the university and internship at boutique hotel, Ava writing a business plan, and a few things about the weather that showed how uncomfortable he was with the silence. "You can use my phone to call her."

Megan shook her head and poured another glass of wine. She was too embarrassed to tell her sisters how her righteous indignation had turned out. She was learning to take care of herself, but she was also learning how impossibly hard it was to be completely on your own.

If she'd had the same opportunities as her sisters, she might have veered from her path and taken another. But the only man she'd ever slept with was sitting across the table and she couldn't leave southern California for her cat-loving aunt's home.

Self-pity felt like quicksand, so Megan grabbed on to the edge of what she could to pull herself out. "Why were you in New York? Stalking my sister too?"

A slow grin spread across his handsome face. "If I was stalking you, you would have been prey long ago. I was researching a textile firm we were thinking of acquiring, so I tracked down Ava while I was there."

"I'm sure you were disappointed to find she didn't need

rescuing. Were you hoping for some of her infamous gratitude?" The problem with having a secret affair was that no one would know they were hurting you by sleeping with your ex. She was even more grateful for Jack Sullivan than before.

"She's your sister."

Megan shrugged. "Your scruples aren't so exacting, and she doesn't know we ever had anything going on. It could happen."

"No."

Megan drank the wine, but it had lost its flavor. She just wanted a hole she could crawl into and hide until her mind thought of a way out. The only option she could think of to protect herself from Brandon and her father was a time machine, but even if they made an app for that, she couldn't afford it. She set down her empty glass and rubbed the back of her neck. The wine was making her melodramatic.

It also made her want revenge. She wanted her father to have to try to sleep someplace he knew he wasn't altogether safe instead of in some beach bungalow, and she wanted Brandon's heart to bleed when he realized what he thought was his never was. She didn't have the first clue where her father might be, and she doubted Brandon cared enough about his current lover to be hurt by her and vice versa. The peroxide junkie rolled through hunky underwear models at a speed that rivaled Ava's collection of former bedmates.

If you don't care, you can't get hurt.

Why hadn't she learned that lesson sooner? Her mind was in overdrive and she couldn't help the answer. Because she'd hoped that Brandon truly cared for her. She knew better, but hope had tricked her into feeling safe when she'd never been in more danger.

The waitress came by with the dessert menu, but Megan was no longer tempted. When Brandon handed over a slew of cash without even looking at the bill, remorse flooded her. The high road might have brought her to a dark place, but she didn't want to derail. If she kept moving, maybe she'd be out of this hell before the devil got his due.

"I'll pay for my half." She took out her wallet and began fingering the bills, hating that they were all singles.

"We talked hotels, so it's a business expense. It's not my money or your money. Does that make you feel better?"

She shook her head and zipped her handbag closed. "Seeing you seems to make me feel worse. Go ahead, take it personally." Her eyes felt heavy but she wouldn't let him see her break, wouldn't let him see how what he'd done made her feel terminally stupid.

"You can't blame yourself for what's happened."

"Oh, I don't. I blame you completely." She was trying to at least. If what Brandon was saying had even a modicum of truth, she might have played a part in her father's downfall. If not for her, Brandon might not have ever bothered to examine what was going on at Carlton hotels, her father might never have decided to take everything and run.

Megan stood and the room spun. She grabbed the back of her chair as her gaze snagged on the empty wine bottle. She could add lush to her impressive resume now.

Brandon took her arm. If he noticed that she'd had too much to drink he didn't let on as he guided her out of the restaurant and into the Escalade. She held herself close to the door and stared out the window, needing to be behind a locked door so she could release the ugly emotions churning within her.

Brandon started the engine, his hands gripping at the steering wheel. "I am sorry about all this, Meg."

"I doubt you know how to be sorry." She leaned her head

against the cool glass of the window and promised herself that someday he would be very, very sorry.

He was either glutton for punishment or completely in love. Brandon tucked the blanket around Megan and crawled back out of the SUV. He'd reclined the seat, but he figured if he moved her she'd wake up as mad as a skunked dog.

Instead, he stood in his garage like some kind of lunatic and watched her sleep. He'd missed that terribly. Megan was a spitfire during her waking hours, but when she dreamed she looked like an angel. She was divinely petite with an ethereal mystery and honest convictions about the rights of the less fortunate. He missed all those things about her, but most of all he ached for the way she used to look up at him.

Her gaze had held nothing but anger and hurt as of late, and he missed the excited joy, the teasing admiration of just a few months ago. Where had that woman gone, and was she too lost to let him bring her back?

He watched her through the windshield, knowing she'd be angrier than ever when she woke up. He hadn't planned on taking her here, but when she'd fallen asleep while he was driving, he took advantage of the opportunity and made it all the way to his Malibu house. There was more to her anger than she was sharing, more than Ava had been able to clue him into, and he wasn't about to let her out of his sight until he figured out what that was.

Not having Megan in his life had driven him to the edge. He'd never considered having a woman watched the way he had her under surveillance, or absconding with her while she slept, but he'd run out of options. Desperation did crazy things to a man. He had to take care of her, needed to make sure she was protected and comfortable. She had no choice but to let him. Going back to the way things had been was no longer an option.

Megan stretched her arms and twisted her head, trying to find a more comfortable position. Her fingers touched leather and her eyes shot open, the inside of Brandon's SUV greeting her through the fog of sleep. Her brain began the slow process of connecting the dots of where she was.

In the waning evening light coming through windows on one side of the garage, she looked around to get her bearings—a three-car garage with a golf cart on one side of the SUV and on the other a Bentley Continental convertible.

Neptune blue. She clenched her teeth as she bolted up and stared closer at the car.

Her car, or it had been before everything had gone down.

She tossed aside the blanket Brandon must have put on her and scrambled out of the SUV, barely taking the time to snatch her handbag from the floor. She ran her hand along the sleek exterior as she stepped to the passenger side and then said a silent prayer that Brandon hadn't set the alarm. She reached inside and flipped open the glove box, a tiny thrill shooting through her when she saw the charging mat she'd left there.

Everything else was there too—the driving moccasins she changed to if her heels were too high, her ebook reader, the braided leather leash, a bag of dog treats and a roll of pooch poop bags. Her heart clenched.

A small sob escaped her before she could rein it in. She quickly schooled her emotions, biting the inside of her cheek, forcing steady breaths. She took her things from the glove box because they were hers. If she'd realized how serious things were with her finances, she would have cleaned out the car before it was towed out of the hotel parking lot. Their cars being seized is what had tipped off the hotel staff, sending them into homelessness.

She looked around the garage again, a sense of familiarity starting to bloom. The Malibu house, right on the beach and perfect for parties. She'd come to one of his infamous parties with Ava when she was much too young to be there, and had set her sights on him then. He was fresh out of military school, eager to make up for all the fun he hadn't been having. His enthusiasm had been as magnetic as his cocksure grin. Every time he turned her down, it made her want him more, so much so that she lost all interest in the boys at school.

Megan's heart squeezed for that idealistic girl who thought she could change the world without it changing her. If she would have known, she might have been able to convince herself Brandon Knight wasn't the man for her. He'd told her as much back then.

She really needed to learn to listen.

Hitching her handbag on her shoulder, she made her way into the house. She couldn't pick a fight with Brandon now. Malibu was at least an hour from Pasadena. There wasn't a way to bus it, she'd have to get a cab, and the entire ride back to the apartment she'd be calculating how many hours she'd have to work to pay for it.

In the laundry room that separated the garage from the house, she slipped off her sneakers and finger combed her hair, hoping she didn't look as exhausted as she felt. She didn't want to show him any more weakness than she already had by falling asleep.

It wasn't her fault she hadn't been able to sleep for more than an hour without being jolted awake by some sound that terrified her. It was just the way things were right now, but not for much longer. Soon she'd have the money to take some computer classes, and then she'd find a job doing administrative work for someone who did fundraising, and eventually she'd be able to direct people with too much money towards the causes she believed in.

It had seemed so much better when she didn't know her sister was an entrepreneur. Sleeping your way to security might not be altogether ethical, but it was damned effective.

Megan pushed open the door to the kitchen, smiling to herself as she took in the empty room. This was a beach house for the Knight family, so it wasn't as done up as their home in Beverly Hills or as modern as Brandon's penthouse. The russet-tinged paint gave the cool granite countertops a cozy feel, the butcher-block island holding the obligatory fruit bowl. The room was women's-magazine perfect, but not designer. She'd always felt comfortable here, probably because over the years she and Brandon had managed to have sex in every room of the house. Usually while there was a party going on. He loved the thrill of being caught, got turned on by seeing her act as if nothing had happened.

It was probably those little thrills that had kept him interested for as long as he had been. As long as she stayed a fantasy, he could escape reality. Once she actually needed him, he wasn't interested and started looking for his excitement elsewhere.

She hoped. It nauseated her to think he'd been sleeping with Gemma while they were together.

She carefully set her bag by the door and cleared her throat. Before she could call out to Brandon, the hollow sound of dog nails scrambling for purchase and tap dancing across the hardwoods thundered down the hall as he ran full bore into the kitchen. She knelt down in anticipation of Money, Brandon's boxer.

He was there all right, trying to climb all over her, but Megan barely noticed. Her entire world had narrowed to one black bundle of fur. She caught Cash, the cockapoo Brandon had given her for her twenty-first birthday, as he leapt for her.

Every wall she'd built to keep herself moving forward crumbled in that instant. She was crying and laughing at the same time, Cash yipping his approval of her return to him. Megan felt every inch of her dog, forever a puppy, making sure he was as perfect as the day she'd left him with Kimberly. It took a while for the excitement of the reunion to calm enough for Megan to notice Brandon too had joined the fray, sitting across from her with Money stretched across his lap.

"Thank you." She clutched her dog to her chest and wiped her eyes with the back of her hand. "It will be hell to give him back to Kimberly."

Brandon leveled his gaze at her. "Kimberly didn't have him."

Megan knit her brow. "She gave him to you? But how did she know—"

"She left him at the kennel last month and headed to Paris. When your credit card was rejected they tried to call you, but you were having your cell-phone issue. They scanned the chip in his ear for another way to find you and found me instead."

She rubbed the soft fur of Cash's ear. "How?"

"I bought him, Megan."

"For me." She held him tighter, panic seizing her. He couldn't possibly want her dog. It was too much, beyond anything else he'd already ripped from her. Her money, her hope, her pride were all his, but she wouldn't let him separate her from the one thing that truly loved her back. Everyone else only cared for her as it suited them, present company included.

She and Cash had a mutual admiration society since she'd first set eyes on him.

"Be glad I didn't make a distinction between what was mine and what was yours. They might have sold him to someone who can take care of him."

"I can take care of him." She wiped at her eyes again, hating the tremor in her voice.

He reached out, laying a hand on her knee. She jerked away, wondering just what she'd do to keep the dog. Probably more than she'd do to actually be able to rewind time like she dreamed about.

"Relax, Meg. I'm not going to let anyone take Cash."

She nodded and squeezed her eyes shut, immediately wishing tears hadn't rolled down her cheeks. She clutched Cash tighter, but he'd had his fill and wriggled away. With reluctance, she let him go. He didn't go far, just into the living room to return with his favorite ball. At least Kimberly had left his things with him when she'd abandoned him.

No, it wasn't her fault. She had a life, one as lacking in responsibility as Megan's had been. She couldn't stay in town just because she had another dog to look after. God, life was unfair sometimes. Megan pulled her knees to her chest and gave herself a good squeeze.

Cash changed everything. It was one thing to surrender Brandon to Gemma Ryan, it was quite another to think of the tramp with her hands on her puppy too. Brandon had made his choice, and in the end she wasn't surprised he couldn't keep it in his pants. Hurt and wrecked and angry and devastated, sure.

Surprised, not so much.

She sat up straighter as her mind wove its way around a new plan, and a slow grin spread across her face. Curling up into a ball of depression and drowning in the quicksand of self-pity wasn't an option. These were the cards she was dealt, and better to play them than fold.

The only way to win the game was to play. She'd judged Ava too harshly in her survival tactics. They'd worked out well for her, so Megan steadied herself to take a page out of her sisters' playbook. After all, it was the only surefire way to get rid of Gemma Ryan once and for all.

Chapter Four

"Do you think I could take a bath? The tub upstairs is divine." Megan stretched her arms over her head, her lush breasts pushing at the thin fabric of her T-shirt. "Of course, I don't have anything to change into. Would you mind if I ran these clothes through the wash?"

Brandon grinned. Now this was his Megan. A sexy minx full of innuendo and ripe with sensual possibility. They'd once used the soaking tub upstairs so thoroughly she'd actually claimed she couldn't get herself out.

He pushed up from the floor and stood, extending his hand to her. "Make yourself at home, babe."

She slipped her hand in his and lust snapped around him like a whip as he pulled her up. She slid right into place, her body skimming his as she stood. He recognized the passionate promise in her gaze. Blood thrummed in his veins, anticipation simmering as her eyes met his.

Her shining blonde hair tumbled over her shoulders, the waves curling about her face. He lifted a finger to her cheek, tucking the loose waves behind one ear and then the other. She really was breathtakingly beautiful, with features fit for the most fairytale of princesses. Before he could think about the repercussions, he moved his hand to the nape of her neck and threaded his fingers in the warm, silken strands. He curled his hand around the back of her head to hold her still, because he couldn't stand for her to turn away now. He lowered his head, hesitating for a split second before his lips found hers.

A bolt of sensation shot through him as the world faded into a whirling haze. With the kiss he tried to show her just how much he'd missed her, how much he hated that he had a hand in what had happened to her family. But as his body went from hot to blazing, he could only think of how long it had been since he'd had her naked.

He skimmed his hands across her soft skin, loving the curve of her waist, the flare of her hips. Her body had always screamed sex to him. He saw her and went hard at the promise of sizzling, wild, mind-blowing sex.

It took nothing but a look and he was ready for anything she had on offer. He moved his hands around to her bottom and pulled her closer, his erection pressing into her belly.

Megan's hands pushed at his shoulders, breaking the kiss. She arched a brow and gave him a naughty smile. "I think I'll take that bath now. Alone."

"Are you sure?"

She gave a coquettish giggle and nodded. "I'll let you know if I need help with anything, but I'm sure I'll be fine."

She stepped back into the laundry room and pulled her shirt over her head. The cream-colored lace edging on her black bra sent his pulse running. She tossed her shirt in the washer and started it up. She stretched for the detergent on the shelf over the machines, but couldn't quite reach.

Thankful for a reason to get close to her again, he made his way into the small space and snagged the container. She gave him a smile as she added soap to the wash, but it was painted on, not genuine like before. He knew he'd pushed too far with the kiss. He just couldn't help himself after so long without her.

"Megan, I know things between us are complicated right now, but—"

"We've always been very uncomplicated, Brandon. Pleasure for pleasure, no responsibilities, no awkward complications." She undid her belt and slid it from the loops, then set it atop the dryer.

"It feels awkward right now."

"That's because we want different things." She unfastened her jeans and slid them over her hips and down her legs. Her blue eyes sparkled as she grinned this time. "You want to take care of me, and I want to take care of myself."

She was the queen of the double entendre. He couldn't count the number of times she'd worked things into conversations at parties and events that had him ditching everything to be alone with her. He cleared his throat and fisted his hands for strength as she bent over to step out of her jeans. Her breasts were amazing, but when she leaned down they were delectable.

After tossing the jeans into the wash, she reached behind her for her bra clasp. Brandon swallowed hard, and wished for time to speed up. He ran his hand over the top of the dryer, his fingers playing with the soft leather of her belt.

"Do you remember that Labor Day party when we tested out the spin-cycle theory?" She shrugged off the bra and added it to the mix.

Brandon could only nod and pray she wanted a repeat performance. Though he didn't remember it being one of their better moments, he'd settle for anything right about now.

"I think that's what's happened to us." She hooked her fingers in her panties and pulled them down. She leaned over and he had to close his eyes. If he watched any more he'd be inside her within ten seconds with no preamble or permission.

"We had fun for a while, but when it came down to it, the cycle ended."

His eyes shot open and he wanted to disagree, but she'd already left the room. He scrambled out in time to watch her shapely bottom sway with each step up the stairs.

Megan made it all the way to the bathroom before her bravado cracked. Her hands shook as she turned the taps for the bath. She and Brandon spent most of their time together naked, but that was before she knew he was spending time that way with Gemma Ryan. Even the woman's name made her shoulders tight. Gemma came from a family with money they didn't earn, just as she had. The difference was that Gemma's family still had both their money and their status, while she had neither.

Brandon loved money, evident by the names he'd given their dogs—though he claimed Cash was named after the man in black, she never actually believed him. She shouldn't have been surprised when he found her dissolving liquidity a turn-off.

And Gemma had lots of boy toys, which meant she had lots of bedroom experience to dazzle Brandon with. Megan had only ever been with him, so if he hadn't done it, neither had she. Maybe Gemma's resume has been the attraction. He wanted someone who knew how to be wicked in ways she'd never even thought of.

Bile burned her throat at the thought of him and the leggy bottle blonde. Her stomach twisted and knotted as she opened drawers, telling herself it wasn't to find evidence that he'd been here with someone else lately.

She braided her hair as she checked the room. Megan couldn't find any evidence that he'd brought the tramp here, even her own bottle of almond bath oil was still tucked in a cabinet.

It was too bad she couldn't find something to stoke her ire.

She was starting to doubt her ability to carry out her plan to seduce Brandon.

Not his willingness, she knew him well enough to know she could have had him on the washing machine long before the spin cycle. She didn't know if she could have sex with someone she wasn't in love with. She couldn't love Brandon anymore, not after what he'd done to her father, and what he'd done with Gemma Ryan.

She poured some of the bath oil into the deep garden tub, the warm water activating the sweet almond scent. From the cabinet beside the shower, she grabbed a white towel and set it on the ledge beside the tub. Sliding into the warm water was the closest thing to heaven she'd experienced in months.

By the time the tub filled enough for her to turn off the taps, Megan realized that while she knew she couldn't love Brandon anymore, she hadn't exactly stopped. The water sloshed around her as she sank deeper, remembering how touched and sweet he'd been all those years ago after he realized a little too late that she was still a virgin.

The next weekend he'd declared a do-over and they'd made love slowly with dozens of candles flickering around his bedroom. Now that was a night to remember.

"I really hope you're thinking about me." His deep voice filled the room and warmed her from the inside, the way it always had. She didn't even startle at the sound.

"I'm thinking this tub is as wonderful as I remembered." She didn't open her eyes, but noticed the room darken. He must have turned off the light.

"I remember a couple of amazing nights that started in this

tub." The water rippled around her, the movement feeling like a faraway caress.

Before she let herself get pulled under by the sensuality of the past, Megan opened her eyes. He'd taken off his shirt so he wore only his jeans as he crouched beside the tub. "Is that why you brought me here? You wanted to have sex and my apartment wasn't doing it for you? Were you too afraid someone might see us at the penthouse?"

Brandon pulled his hand from the water as if it burned him. "I wasn't the one who wanted our relationship to be a secret, Meg. That was all you."

"You loved it though. The secrecy and sneaking around made it hot for you." She met his gaze, hating the mocking stare he gave her.

"It was hot for you too. I am not the big bad wolf in this, and you are not an innocent little red riding hood. My mistake was in not pushing you to be honest with your family about us years ago. That's where I went wrong."

"Nope, that's not it." She pulled her knees to her chest and wrapped her arms around her legs. Every time she thought of where things went wrong, her mind supplied her with a montage of images of Gemma Ryan plastered to his face. "We've seen how the media has picked apart the relationships of our friends. Keeping things private was the right choice. Can you imagine the press if they'd known about us when your little deal went down? It would have been absolutely brutal."

"And this isn't? I've spent two months thinking you'd chosen your father and the islands over me, and then I find out you never left, but couldn't be bothered to even let anyone know that you're all right? These last few weeks have been torture, knowing you were working yourself like crazy and that you've lumped all your anger over what happened on me."

"I can't absolve you of your guilt. You did a bad thing, a couple of them."

"No, I—"

The water rippled as Megan raised her hand out of the water and held it up. "Stop making excuses for what happened. You had your reasons for blindsiding me. I'm never going to think they're any good. And in light of what's happened since, you don't make a very strong case."

He paced the bathroom and pushed his hands through his hair, creating a disheveled disarray that reminded her of what he looked like in the morning. Her heart squeezed with longing to see him that way again. Her love for him wasn't a switch she could flip or a dial she could turn down. He'd hurt her horribly, betrayed her completely, and yet her soul still held on to him as if he were the prince she'd always hoped he would become.

He turned to face her and put his hands on his hips. "What do I have to say to get you to see I didn't do any of this to hurt you?"

"I never thought you did. You just didn't think outside yourself enough to realize that it would." She leaned forward and pulled the drain, the gurgling sound of the disappearing water filling the silence.

Megan both craved and hated what she was about to do. A part of her wanted to be with Brandon and feel alive and happy the way she used to, but another part hated the idea that by being with him she'd be bartering her body for the security he could provide. She wished she had more options, but it seemed options were the only thing she had less of than money.

She couldn't leave without her dog, and she couldn't take him with her. Animals weren't allowed at her apartment complex and she couldn't afford any place else. She was as trapped as Wendy from the coffee shop. When she found a way out of this, she'd also find a way for the Carlton Houses to accept pets. Her fundraising abilities had slipped since she'd become persona non grata with the charitable set, but it wouldn't be like that forever. Now that she knew how desperate and trapped it felt, she'd do whatever it took to make pets an option for the women at the shelters.

Just like she'd do whatever she had to now to keep Brandon from his new lover, and keep herself with Cash. She hoped that someday the ends would justify the means.

As the water swirled down the drain with the remains of her stubborn pride, Megan pushed up and stood in the tub, letting the water sluice down her bare body. Even in the dim room, it caught Brandon's attention immediately.

She reached for the towel, and then stood up tall, pulling her shoulders back as she started patting her body dry. She could do this because he would make it easy. Just like always, she'd lay out the invitation and he'd be on her before she could say RSVP.

This was it. The escape hatch from the disaster her life had become. All she had to do was give him an inch and he'd take her all the way back to their old life. But her hands were shaking and her heart was racing and neither was conducive to temptation.

She closed her eyes and took a deep breath, searching for the courage to seduce him. She'd done it countless times before, but then she'd needed nothing from him.

"Megan?" His tone was low and husky, a sound so familiar and comforting her eyes drifted open. It really was like going back in time as he held out his hand and helped her step out of the tub. The bathmat was soft beneath her feet as she let him take the towel from her hands and slowly, oh so slowly, dry her skin.

In a few more minutes she might not need the towel. Heat flared within and she figured the water would simply turn to steam. She looked down at Brandon, his broad shoulders and solid chest and desire spiraled within her.

He'd always oozed sex appeal. It was what had drawn her to him long before she had any chance of being able to handle it. He had a sexual energy that was as tempting as it was intense and overwhelming.

And it was exactly what she needed.

As he crouched down to dry her legs, she spread them wider, her skin aware of his every move. His face was shadowed as he looked up at her, a grin curving his full lips. He flung the towel on the floor as he stood.

As if by magic, he managed to lift her into his arms. On instinct, she wrapped her arms around his neck, the fingers of one hand pushing through the shorn hair at the nape. He carried her into the bedroom and laid her back on the pillows of the bed. He joined her before she could think, nuzzling his face against her throat as his hands caressed her body.

"Whenever I smell almonds," he whispered, his hot breath making her squirm, "I think about the time you got that kiddie pool and we slathered each other with bath oil and made love over—" he licked her neck, the scene playing in her head like a movie, "—and over—" he swirled his tongue against her throat as his hands slid up to cover her breasts, "—and over."

She moaned and reached for him, the stubble on his face rough against her cheek as she dragged his mouth to hers. She kissed him as if he were water in the middle of the desert.

She felt exactly as she used to—wild and free and hungry for him.

She flattened one palm against his chest, feeling the thundering beat of his heart beneath the wall of muscle. He rolled her aching nipples between his fingers and bolts of electricity coursed to her center. Her mouth opened beneath the power of his lips and all her apprehensions about being with him vanished.

He kissed, he suckled and cherished her lips and tongue, driving her mad to the point where she could almost come from the kiss itself. It was a skill he'd perfected over the years and she'd never been so glad to be on the receiving end of his talents. Her wanton body tingled as his kisses crept down her throat. It was amazing how fast she'd gone from unsure to more than ready, but Brandon had years of practice and played her body like a talented musician.

His tongue drew lazy circles around her nipple before he turned his head and rubbed his stubbled cheek on the sensitive tip. He rewarded her with a soothing lick before he pulled the nub into his mouth and flicked it with his tongue until her toes curled into the mattress. When he repeated the performance on the other breast, she moaned his name in pleasure.

He slid his hand down her belly and between her legs, finding her wet and ready for him. She heard the zipper of his jeans release and opened eyes she hadn't realized she closed. A precious shred of caution slipped through her wild reckless desires.

"Do you have any condoms?" Her tummy flipped, both wanting him to have a stash and not wanting him to be prepared because of what that would mean.

"Why? We haven't used them in years." His voice was gravelly and thick, but his expression was crestfallen.

"The pill was an unnecessary expense, considering." She'd only stopped using condoms because she'd thought they were exclusive. That had been a condition of not sending him to the store for more that Christmas Eve four years ago.

His eyelids drooped and his mouth twisted into a near pout. She had to smile at the wistful way he dragged his gaze over her body. The pause in the action was enough to allow her brain to start working again. Was he not using protection with Gemma, or had he just not thought to bring any with him? Maybe he hadn't wanted to have sex with her until she pulled her naked stunt. Maybe this wasn't—

"Oh no you don't." Brandon rolled on top of her and laced his fingers in hers. "Don't you leave me again. You were right here with me and I have missed you."

"Have you?" She ran her calf over his jean-clad leg, once again allowing herself to slip into the illusion that he was telling the truth.

He moved their hands out to the side and pushed up to look down into her eyes. "Easily the worst months of my life."

He delivered the words with such honest conviction that her heart squeezed for him, a voice too much like hers answered back, "Mine too."

Soft lips found hers again, savoring her at first, before she struggled against his grip so that she could use her hands to devour him completely. He pulled back, and then rested his forehead against hers.

"Do you remember when somebody dared Ava not to have sex for forty days, and you thought it would be a good idea to play along?" A wicked grin tugged at the corner of his lips, full and wet from her kisses.

"Why are we talking about my sister and her boyfriend?"

"That was Sullivan?" Megan nodded. "Huh. Okay, but follow me here. We did make it for almost a week before you broke down and jumped me in the shower."

"You wish."

"I really do. But seriously, we managed. In fact, it was kind of fun to be creative." He dipped his head and gave her nipple a slow lick.

The naughty laugh she gave spurred him on. She relaxed into his ministrations, her dirty mind thinking of ways she could still accomplish her plan without him realizing what she was about. She wanted to feel like her former self, but she didn't want to have to deal with the confrontations living that life again would lead to. Running her hands over the firm muscles of Brandon's back felt delicious and right, reality had no place in it.

He kissed his way down her belly and the sexual tension that had been arcing between them for weeks spiraled and focused itself into a delicious ache between her legs. He ran his hands over her hips and down the outside of her thighs.

When he reached her knees, he parted her legs and moved between them. He placed open-mouthed, warm kisses everywhere he knew she liked—the back of her knees, where her knee met her inner thigh, the juncture of her leg and torso. Everywhere he touched, her skin tingled until she was completely intoxicated from his attentions.

By the time he gave her sex a long, slow lick, she was pounding on the door of release. She rocked her hips against him and he anchored her steady with his hands. She reached down with one hand and threaded her fingers into his hair, the short ends prickling the sensitized skin of her palm. Every nerve ending danced in anticipation of her climax.

With her free hand, she squeezed her breast, then rolled her nipple between her fingers, loving how the sensation travelled right where Brandon was. He slipped a finger into her, curling it towards her clit as he focused his mouth there. Her hips lifted from the mattress as the sensations crashed together like breaker waves, sending her higher and higher until every muscle in her body relaxed in sweet release.

While her body drifted through delicious aftershocks, he teased her with lingering licks until she shifted her hips away from him. He kissed his way back up her body, tucking her head under his chin and stroking his fingers over her scalp and through her hair.

When she roused herself from the post-orgasm bliss, she smiled up at him. "You look pretty pleased with yourself."

"And you look pretty and pleased." He kissed the top of her head.

"I'm not buying your selfless intentions. I know you far too well for that." With purposeful slowness, she slid her hand over the planes of his chest and ridges of his abdomen to toy with the open front of his jeans.

"I never claimed to be a martyr, but I definitely enjoyed myself."

Through the thin material of his tented boxer briefs, she stroked the sizable proof. As she stroked him, he let out a low groan she could feel against her head. She turned and kissed the taut skin where his neck met his shoulder, excited by all she was about to do. She tasted the salt on his bare skin, nipping with her teeth and then alternating soothing licks with sharp sucks of her mouth. He either liked it, or he didn't care what she did while her hand explored him over his briefs.

It felt wicked and naughty.

It gave her the control back she'd been lacking for far too long. When she was sure she'd managed what she intended, Megan pulled his penis through the opening of his briefs, amazed by how long and thick he appeared. With his black briefs still on his body, his cock appeared like an art sculpture, ready to be praised and enjoyed. A near overwhelming desire to mount him and take her pleasure anew washed over her. A few short months ago she would have, but now she had to play the game a few steps ahead and not in the moment.

She lifted her gaze to meet his and licked her lips. The fire of passion burned his eyes when she wrapped her hand around his girth and started to stroke him again. She fought to stay in control of the moment, but her disobedient imagination started spinning thoroughly naughty ideas for how they might both get off again. It was tricky not to slip back into old habits, especially when he looked down at her with such potent sexuality that she felt every part the nymphet her body wanted to be.

He dipped his head, stubble brushing the smooth skin of her cheek as he whispered, "I would give anything for a condom right now."

"Then it's too bad I don't have one. There's no telling what I could get out of you." She squeezed him and he jerked in her hand. With his face so close to hers she could see the warm brown of his eyes, the deep richness that always sent her pulse racing. Being this close reminded her of the times when she'd felt as if she knew secrets about him that no one else thought to guess. Now it was true, but in an entirely different way than she'd hoped.

"Oh, Meg, there is nothing I wouldn't give you." He closed his eyes and gently brought his lips to hers. The intimacy of the moment made her heart lurch and her eyes started to prickle. If only he'd given her the one thing she'd always wanted, her entire world would be different and it wouldn't have cost him a dime.

She moved her mouth to his neck, and then his collar bone, not wanting the familiarity of his kiss. If he could continue to play her while they were in bed together, then he had been playing her all along. Sadness washed over her as she continued to kiss her way down his body.

The thing about the last time you make love with your lover, is that rarely do you realize it is the last time. If she had, she would have done something more exciting than lingerie after dinner.

This time would be the very last chance she ever had to love him. She wanted to make it good, as close to unforgettable as she could manage, and still accomplish her secondary goal. She laved his nipples, admiring the leanness of his body. She savored each plane and ridge of muscle, her hands and mouth traveling the path they knew so well. She found the firm edge where the muscles of his torso met his hip. The smooth skin was soft beneath her lips and she pressed her teeth deeper into his flesh by slow degrees. With her hands, she pulled at his jeans and boxer briefs. Brandon was so enthralled he helped her rid him of his clothing while she made sure her own brand of damage was done. She wrapped her hand around his erection again, stroking him while she pulled the sensitive skin of his hip into her mouth.

He groaned and bucked into her hand, satisfying the primal part of her that wanted, needed to know her power. Content that she'd done what she'd set out to, she moved on.

Wrapping her hand around the base of him, she played with his balls and trailed her tongue along the sensitive underside of his shaft. He hissed at the attention and tangled his hands in her hair.

She ran her tongue along the swollen head of him until a tangy bead glistened at the tip of him. Then she took him in her mouth, her lips stretching around him while she flicked the underside with her tongue. As she eased him deeper into her mouth, she softened her tongue and sucked, using her experience with what he liked just as he had done for her.

Her body began to tingle anew as she began to slide him slowly in and out of her mouth, using her hand to massage the lower half of his shaft. Her mouth and hand worked in practiced harmony as memories of other times they'd been together this way flooded her mind. Scenes from the balcony of his penthouse, her car, his shower, the stairway of the Hansen Auditorium where they'd been attending some ridiculously long fundraiser and she hadn't been able to stand the way women were swirling around him.

Brandon fisted his hands in her hair, his breathing becoming rough pants as his balls tightened and his legs tensed. Megan hadn't realized she'd increased her pace as the memories played through her mind like naughty movies. She absorbed his growing fervor, her boldness growing in time with his pleasure. His hips rocked to the same rhythm as her mouth and she released his balls, pressing that hand between her own legs to relieve the pressure building there.

It all felt so incredibly good, so amazingly right, that she knew her own orgasm wouldn't be far behind his. His fingers clenched in her hair and she knew he was closing in, so she rubbed her fingers against her swollen clit, chasing down her climax as she brought his to him. His hips jerked and shook, so she stroked and sucked harder, her heart hammering in her chest in eager anticipation.

Brandon roared her name as he spurted down her throat. She swallowed quickly, her hands starting to shake as her stomach fluttered and hot bolts of sensation coursed outwards from her core. She released him and rolled to the side, lying beside him as she caught her breath.

In a moment she would have to get up and dress, grab Cash and tell Brandon to take her back to the apartment. If

Chapter Five

"I need you to take me back to Pasadena." Megan's warm hand curled around his biceps. Brandon had been listening to her bustle about the bedroom, refusing to open his eyes. Last night had been a doorway back to the way things were, and he'd bolted it shut. He was never going back through it.

"Brandon, wake up. I have a meeting at ten."

His stomach tightened and he opened one eye. He did not want to let her go, not yet, not ever. He wasn't deluded enough to think that things were back to normal, but at least they were moving in the right direction.

Megan sat on the bed, fully dressed and looking better than anyone should in her jeans and T-shirt. He cleared the sleep from his throat and wished she'd woken him up in her usual under-the-covers manner.

"Take your car." He stretched his arms out, bringing one behind his head and the other around to her.

"The Bentley is yours now, not mine." She shifted away from him, clutching Cash to her chest, the dog's Fendi bag of toys already over her shoulder. "You brought me here. I need you to take me back."

"No way. You're not going to play this game with me again." He sat up and reached for her, but she stood, still holding on to the dog as if fifteen pounds of puppy were the answer to all her problems. Cash stared at him as if he should know what to do.

"I didn't ask to come here and I can't take Cash on the bus unless he's in his carrier, and I can't find one anywhere."

"You were going to leave and not even say anything to me?" He tossed back the blanket and stood, his heart hammering in his chest. Two minutes ago he'd thought he'd managed to get his world back in order, and now one small woman had turned it completely upside down. Again.

"I have nothing to say to you." She gave him a haughty smile and kept her gaze on his face, only slipping once to check out his morning erection.

"Try again."

"I can't stay here. I have a fundraising meeting that I need to be at."

He studied her for a moment, but he couldn't pin down how she felt. He should be able to read her, but she had on such a front he couldn't get past it to discern scared from angry, hurt from confused. "You need to be here. We've got to figure us out because I can't keep going on like this."

"There is no us, Brandon. You made sure of that." A hurt flickered in her eyes that hit him like a kick to the balls. "The Carlton Houses are struggling without my family's backing, so I have a brainstorming session with the directors to think of some other ways to keep things running. It's actually important business, not a grown man having a temper tantrum because he wants what he can't have."

He gave her an aren't-you-funny smile. "I'll write a check. You're not leaving."

"I don't want your guilt money."

"Don't let pride get in your way, Megan. Like you said, the Carlton Houses are actually important, unlike a grown woman having a fit because she can't have things exactly the way she wants them. If the program needs the money, it doesn't matter where it comes from. It matters to me that we talk this through without needing to trade insults."

"Go ahead and send your check. If you won't take me to Pasadena, I'll call the car service that will let me take Cash, and not have money for rent next week." She hitched her bag higher on her shoulder and lifted her chin.

"You don't need rent money. You're staying here." Brandon shook his head and rounded the bed to where she stood. Megan took a step back, so instead of reaching for her, he reached out and tried to comfort the confused dog in her arms.

"Like hell." Fury flashed in her gaze. "I will not be the piece of ass you hide away in Malibu. I don't care how far you think I've fallen now that I don't have my father's money, I am still better than that."

He blinked, unsure where her anger was coming from. He held up his hands to stall out her attack. "You're the one hiding. That's what Pasadena is, you know. I'm going to take a shower. If you want me to take you to your meeting, I will. And then after we'll talk until I understand why it is you think I'm the monster in the story of your life."

He strode into the bathroom, slamming the door behind him. He turned on the taps and stared down at the fluffy white towel on the cold tile floor. How in the world could one woman be so hot for him one minute and despise him a few short hours later? He'd been sleeping in the interim, so there was no way he could have done anything to rouse her ire.

There was something going on in that pretty little head of hers, and he was going to find out what it was if it killed them both. He showered quickly, his mind spinning through what to say to her next and discarding options at rapid speed.

Brandon turned off the shower and reached for a towel. He dragged it roughly over his body, wincing as it scratched at his neck. He shifted, then winced again when it scratched at his hip. He glanced down, his eyes widening as he took in the bite mark mere inches from where it could have really hurt. He stepped to the mirror and inspected a world-class hickey on his neck.

Without stopping to think, he stormed to the door and threw it open. "What the hell did you do to me?" he screamed to an empty room.

Since Brandon told her to take the car, Megan didn't think it was stealing. At least not in the most technical sense, hopefully not in the legal sense either. She shuddered to think of him having her arrested and then posting bail just to ensure she had to stay within his reach. She wouldn't put it past him, wouldn't put anything past him anymore.

She stroked Cash's soft head and leaned back in the padded leather desk chair, quietly relieved that she wouldn't have to go back to the apartment tonight. When she'd collected her things, she'd come back to the car to find a cluster of teenage boys eyeing it. She doubted she'd spent ten minutes in the apartment, but that seemed to be all it took for them to recognize the opportunity.

With Cash, she'd have to stay at the Carlton House. Evie was not happy about having a dog in the building again. Megan completely understood why the director would think it sent the wrong message, and she'd probably spend all her tips paying one of the women to watch him while she worked, but she didn't see that she had a choice.

If she left him at the apartment during the night, he'd be scared by all the noises and bark, getting her evicted. How she was going to sleep during the afternoons with all the bustle of the house, she didn't know. But then she barely managed to sleep at the apartment anyway, so she supposed it wouldn't be much different.

On the other hand, she'd slept beautifully in Malibu. Her body still hummed with barely requited satisfaction, but she would not give in to her baser desires. She made it so that Brandon would have trouble hopping from her bed to his new girlfriends', and that was going to have to be enough. Hopefully he'd get the message that she knew about his little fling and leave her the hell alone.

Away from him, she knew just how despicable he was, but for some reason whenever he was around, her love for him blurred the edges of what he'd done. It must have been like this for her mother. Experiencing first-hand the blinding pull of love showed how her mother could continue to stay with a man who routinely cheated on her, but it didn't make it any easier to understand. It was hard not to buy into Brandon's lies, but it was possible.

"Megan, we have a problem." Evie stood in the doorway of her own office, her arms crossed over her chest. "When I asked to push the meeting back until this afternoon it was because of a family, one I'd really like to place here. It's a single mom and her two daughters. They lost their apartment on the first of the month and have been living in their car."

Megan nodded, her stomach feeling hollow. "They can have the room. I really just need someone to watch Cash while I'm at work for a few weeks until I can find a new place." She swallowed hard and pinned on a smile.

"I don't like the idea of having to be responsible for your dog. We have so much going on here."

"It's an easy way for someone to make money. Besides, I

work at night. He'll probably be asleep anyway."

Evie sank into the worn sofa in the corner of the room. "I want to help you, Megan, I do. But isn't there someone else who could watch him?"

Brandon flashed in her mind, but she shook her head to dispel the image. Yes, Cash would be safe with Brandon, but she might not get him back. She had dozens of so-called friends she'd be able to call once her phone finished charging, but she doubted any of them would want to help her. She had no one to depend on but herself, which was a hard place to be since she had an animal who depended on her.

"Evie, I want there to be a Carlton House that takes animals." When the other woman opened her mouth, Megan held up her hand. "Hear me out. This isn't just about me and Cash. By the time we get this program running, I know I'll have figured out a better way to take care of him. But how many times do we see women who won't leave bad situations because of pets? Or families who would rather stay in their car than here because of a dog? There needs to be an option for them."

Compassion filled her dark gaze. "It's not that simple. There are insurance issues and the other guests to consider. We don't want someone who is afraid of dogs or allergic to cats to feel unwelcome."

"That's why I think it should only be available at one of the houses, not all of them. The directors communicate every day, so we should be able to make adjustments. The Carlton Houses fill the cracks in the system to keep people from falling through. This is just another way to do that."

"And the added insurance? Megan, we don't have enough money to make our operating budgets for much longer after the holidays. We need to focus on holding on to what we have, not growing our expenses. If we can't figure out fundraising—"

"Are you starting without us?" Susan Mowery, the plump brunette who ran the Burbank shelter entered the room, followed by the directors from Santa Monica and Glendale.

Megan stared at the two women who followed the directors into the small room, her pulse quickening with recognition.

Jordana Knight's presence couldn't be a coincidence. Brandon's mother was the grande dame of the charity set, but she'd never taken passing notice of the Carlton Houses before. Either Brandon had called her in to help, or to take over completely.

Likely the latter because with her, in a white bandeau mini dress held up only by the audacity of her fake breasts, was Gemma Ryan. Megan looked her over from her sparkly Jimmy Choo sandals to the blonde highlights and lowlights fighting for dominance atop her head. The girl was a hot mess, and a thousand times more suited to Brandon than Megan would ever be.

Knowing how much they deserved each other did nothing to quell the queasiness in her stomach or how her skin prickled with sweat. She still wanted to punch Gemma in her collagen-injected mouth. If not for Cash on her lap, she might have, no matter the cost. What did she have to lose anymore, really?

"Isn't this great?" Susan grinned from ear to ear as she settled onto the couch. "Mrs. Knight called this morning to offer to help with fundraising. I'm so excited to get a plan in place so we won't be in a panic next year."

Megan swallowed and pasted on a smile. Her heart beat an urgent rhythm in her chest. *Run, as fast as you can and as far as you can get.*

Brandon must have called his mother, and what was worse, he probably called in Gemma as payback for the marks she'd left on his body. The treachery of his games cut her to the quick. Maybe she should run, because obviously he was coming after her, and he wasn't about to stop until she had nothing at all. If she got in the car right now, she could make it to Oregon by breakfast tomorrow. Let Brandon say she stole the car. In Oregon, Briana or her aunt could post bail. Though with her aunt's cat collection, she couldn't bring Cash. She held the dog tighter, her mind screaming for an escape, but she couldn't see a clear way out.

"Megan," Jordana Knight said, standing tall in her unforgiving leather blazer and slim pencil skirt. The statuesque brunette was pure sophistication and glamour. "It's lovely to see you."

"And you. I'm surprised you have the time to help us. The holiday season is always packed with functions for your causes." She looked up at the older woman, trying to read an expression that showed nothing at all. Was this the cavalry bent on rescue, or the infantry on a mission to destroy the last thing she had? There was no way of knowing.

"I make time for what's important." Her dark gaze, so like Brandon's dipped from Megan's face to Cash, and back again. "If the Carlton Houses are in trouble, I have some ideas for how we can turn things around."

"Me too," Gemma chimed in, entirely too eager for Megan's liking. She didn't know Gemma well, though they'd gone to the same exclusive private school. Gemma had always been a little too boy crazy to make many friends. Megan wondered just how crazy it would make her to learn where Brandon was last night and how thoroughly he'd enjoyed himself. "There are some simple things we can do to give the organization a quick PR makeover."

"Like what?" Evie asked, before Megan had a chance to tell Gemma what she could do with her ideas.

"Renaming the different houses."

"Absolutely not." Megan stood, her pulse thundering in her ears. "I'm not going to let you erase decades of dedication and support."

"Megan, you need to listen." Jordana's hand on her arm was the only thing that stopped her from saying more, or from knocking the twit backwards out of the small room. "No one is discounting the effort your mother put into starting this to honor your great-grandmother. You just need to be realistic about what is best for the women you help. You will not get a single sizable contribution as long as Carlton is connected to the organization."

Megan shook off her hand. "You want me out?"

Jordana shook her head. "That's not what I'm saying at all. You are key to the consistency of the organization. That you're here speaks to the resiliency of women, which is what this is all about. Think about this—why are they called Carlton Houses?"

"Because there are women who slip through the cracks and don't know how to accomplish what my great-grandmother did. My mother founded the charity and my family has been the primary supporter since inception."

The older woman nodded. "So wouldn't it be better if this were Amanda's House? We could name another after your grandmother."

Evie stood and came to stand beside Megan. "I like it," she said softly.

"You see?" Gemma pressed her hands together in glee. "Then the fundraiser will be a rededication event. You won't seem so desperate."

"We are not desperate." Megan's decibel level belied her words, but she didn't care. She couldn't stand to be put down by the woman sleeping with Brandon.

"Ladies, will you excuse us for a moment?" Jordana Knight gave a look to the others in the room that sent the five women scurrying. When they were alone, she crossed her arms over her chest and stared at Megan for long moments.

Megan met the gaze, not wanting to back down. If they wanted to force her out, she'd go kicking and screaming. She might not have been able to do a thing to stop the financial melee her father had started, but she could put the brakes on destroying this legacy.

The older woman let out a slow sigh and her gaze flickered to the dog and back to Megan. "You need help with this. These shelters are too important for you to let pride get in the way."

"I will not let anyone undo what my mother built."

"That's fair, but Amanda was not born a Carlton and neither was your great-grandmother. No one is trying to take away the tribute to them, but in this community Carlton is synonymous with thief. No one will willingly hand anything with the name Carlton more money when they think he still owes them."

Megan's eyes closed as the argument registered and her stomach sank. Jordana was right. Donations had stopped cold along with the monthly support her parents had provided. They'd been running on reserve funds ever since and it wasn't going to last much longer. They had to do something, or in addition to losing the hotel chain her great-grandmother had built from a run-down boarding house, they'd lose the homes they'd opened in her honor to shelter women from the storms of life.

She opened her eyes and nodded, her voice shaking as she spoke. "I won't work with Gemma."

Jordana blinked. "Why not? She does amazing PR work for a lot of different foundations. She has wonderful contacts that could really help this campaign."

"My reasons are petty, and I don't want to have to see her." Or have to hear about how amazing and wonderful she was.

"I admire your honesty." Her quiet laugh brought a smile to Megan's face. "I'm curious about something else though. Why has my son had your dog for the last month?"

Megan started, a lie to cover the truth forming on her lips. It had become so natural to keep her relationship with Brandon to themselves, her first instinct was to keep up the charade. But since Brandon was with Gemma, a girl who'd attached herself to his mother, there was nothing to hide anymore.

"I wasn't sure where I'd end up, so Cash has been bounced around a bit. But he's back with me now."

Every time he moved, the collar of his shirt scratched against the hickey Megan had left on his neck. To make matters worse, her other love bite was exactly where his jeans creased when he sat. It wouldn't bother him at all if he were naked and she was here the same way.

He shifted in the chair, his jeans growing too tight yet again. After last night, he seemed to have a permanent semi, and if he didn't get Megan beneath him soon he'd surely go mad. Not that he was altogether sane right now.

"Danny!" he bellowed to his empty office. No doubt the administrative assistants between their offices cringed, but he was beyond caring. When he'd arrived this morning, Danny's people had already lost track of Megan. He knew part of that was his fault, having spirited her away to Malibu, but if he didn't know where she was, he wanted someone to.

"Dude," Danny said as he wheeled himself into the room. "We have an intercom. Stop being a Neanderthal and use it."

"Where is she?" His foot tapped against the floor like a woodpecker on speed.

"Pasadena Carlton House. They've tagged her car, so she won't be able to go anywhere in it without being tracked."

The tension in his shoulders eased. He'd been panicked all morning that she'd run further away. He'd even called his mother with news the charity was in trouble to make sure someone set eyes on her today.

If the Carlton Houses really were struggling, his mother would know how to fix things. She knew millions of ways to separate rich people from their money. It was a family tradition of sorts, he and his father collected money and she doled it out to those who needed it. Really, his story was Robin Hood, not the Big Bad Wolf. Why couldn't Megan see that?

Danny leaned forward. "Are you going to tell me what the real deal is with Megan?"

"Yeah, that's what I need to know too." Gemma Ryan flounced into the office, tossing her oversized handbag on the leather couch. "She refuses to let me help with the campaign at her shelters."

Brandon knit his brows together. "Why would you want to?"

"Your mother asked me to help." As she spoke, she flittered her hands about like twitching butterflies. "I think she knows I'm stressed out and this would be a great distraction. But instead it was all, 'Great ideas, Gemma. You can go now.' Megan was openly rude to me. It's like the Carlton's lost their manners along with their money."

Danny rubbed his nose, his gaze moving from Brandon to Gemma and back again. "You sent your mommy? How old are you?"

"What?" Brandon rubbed his cheek, stubble scratching his

fingers. "She said the organization was having funding trouble. There's no one better to help her."

"Dude, you sent your mommy." Danny began to chuckle.

"Stop saying it like that. I needed to know what they needed to stay afloat."

Gemma huffed and perched a hip on the glass-topped desk. "I don't know why you're helping her at all. She's not very nice. Me on the other hand, you could help me and it wouldn't cost you a thing."

"Oh yeah, you're a real peach." Danny shook his head. "Every nice girl wants to insult the concept of marriage by tying the knot with an even richer man who won't bother her for three hundred and sixty five days so she can inherit a mint, and then let her go without getting his hands on any of her assets." He leered at Gemma in a way that wasn't entirely gentlemanly.

She straightened up. "This was not my idea. My grandfather wanted to make sure I didn't marry for money, he just had a bad way of insuring that didn't happen, and a wonky timeline for it."

"And you have some pretty exacting criteria. I can't find a guy in all of California who I don't think has a reason to take half of everything when you toss him aside next year. Except him." He tilted his head towards Brandon.

"Oh no, no, no. I have my own problems, and this—" he swirled his hand in the air, "—this would make everything much worse. You do it."

"She doesn't want to ride around on my lap, if you know what I mean. I think it's you she wants."

Gemma stomped her foot. "I am in the room! Why is everyone looking at me like I'm trash today?"

Danny shrugged, his gaze lingering on her chest.

"You wouldn't know style if it smacked you in your block head." She grabbed her handbag and slung it over her shoulder. "You—" she pointed at Brandon, "—you need to stop feeling so damned guilty about the Carlton sisters. If Megan doesn't want your help, take her at her word and she'll get what's coming to her." She spun on her stiletto heel and pointed at Danny. "And as for you, mister know-it-all, I'm calling your bluff. You and me, New Years Eve, Las Vegas. Not because I like you, or I feel sorry for you being in that chair, but because if you do screw me, Brandon will pay me back."

She shook her head, her blonde bob waving about her cheeks. "You men make everything far too complicated." She sashayed out of the office as if she'd just solved the problem of world peace.

Danny cleared his throat. "You should have asked her what to do about your Megan problem. Since she has an answer for everything."

No way was he letting Gemma into his personal life, especially if Megan already had a problem with her. "You're just mad because you're usually the one with all the answers."

Danny's lips quirked as he grinned. "You want to know what I think you should do about Megan?"

She'd kept only one dress, and everyone had seen it before. Megan held out the black lace over cream dress and wondered if it still fit. After a lifetime of struggling to stay within a size of her smaller sisters, she was managing it by the simple task of not eating enough. It made her tired and cranky, but she could probably fit into the designer sample sizes that were sent to her friends in the hopes the celebutantes might be photographed in them. If Jordana really did expect her to show her face at the major events this season, then Megan would need to make nice with some of her old classmates. That, or become the talk of the town by wearing the same tired dress over and over.

Megan sighed, wishing she didn't have to parade herself before the benefactors of the city, didn't have to risk seeing Brandon and Gemma together. He hadn't tried to contact her in the last two days, but she figured he was just biding his time, waiting for a chance to strike when it would be deadly and not just scarring.

After working at the bar last night and a long shift at the coffee shop this morning, the only thing she wanted was a few hours of sleep. Instead, she'd had to turn down a shift at the bar she couldn't afford to miss for a party that would last until she had to start brewing coffee in the morning.

Not that she'd stay that long. She'd put in an appearance, let the rumor mill start swirling, and get out long before it could grind her into dust. She'd probably have to do the same thing over and over every weekend until the fundraising party the Saturday before Christmas. Four long weekends of sheer torture. She hoped it would be worth enough to keep the houses running until her sisters could help her think of what to do next.

Talking with them had been an exercise in caution. Ava was so excited about her new business venture and Briana was busy with school, and Megan hadn't wanted to weigh them down with her issues. She kept her side of the conversation strictly on what she'd been doing with the Carlton Houses, and that they weren't going to be called that much longer. Both of her sisters thought it was a lovely idea to name them after women who'd helped so many others.

Since her sisters hadn't balked at the idea, Megan knew she'd reacted to Gemma, not the concept. She resigned herself to changing the names of the centers and hoped that Jordana's idea to let two big contributors choose names of the remaining homes would bring in the capital they all needed.

Cash scurried about her feet, probably wondering if she'd fallen asleep standing up. He never seemed to know what to do with her while they were in the apartment together. He wanted to play, she wanted to sleep. Megan smiled at his inherent happiness and danced around him for a bit to get her energy going before she changed out of her standard jeans and long sleeve T-shirt for something from her former life.

She'd kept this dress not for itself, but for the stilettos that matched it. They were the most spectacular shoes she'd ever owned, and she hadn't wanted to part with them when she'd sold everything else to make the deposits on this hovel of an apartment. She wouldn't miss it a bit when she left.

As soon as she knew the Carlton Houses were stable financially, she was going to head towards one of her sisters and away from Brandon Knight. When she did manage to get any sleep, he was the first thing that drifted into her mind. And he was always naked and willing, and if it weren't for Cash waking her up, she'd probably have called him begging to see him by now. She'd thought of using returning the car as an excuse, but she hadn't trusted herself, and so she was still borrowing it.

The entire predicament really made her feel for her mother. She couldn't help but wonder why her parents had stuck together now, when a scandal like this would have pulled even the closest of couples apart. She didn't understand it, but now that she'd personally experienced the pull towards a man who'd burned you so badly the scars might never heal, she could at least empathize. Her sisters weren't so forgiving.

Megan applied makeup for the first time in weeks and

finger combed through her hair, hoping the loose curls looked purposeful. The only mirror in the apartment was barely big enough for her to see her face, so she hoped for the best as she slipped on the dress, stockings and heels. If being seen by her former friends was as mortifying as she feared, at least Evie would be with her. Megan had convinced her to come to the symphony soiree because she couldn't stand the thought of going alone.

She buttoned her coat and scooped up Cash, grabbing her handbag and keys on the way out. She stalled on the stairs when she saw the crowd of teens hovering around her car. She beeped the alarm, which usually had them walking away, but today they stayed, one of them leaning on the trunk. It made Cash bark like crazy as she did her best to ignore them as she climbed in the car, pretending she didn't hear the coarse words they threw her way.

Her heart hammered in her chest as she locked the doors and drove away. She couldn't blame them for what they thought, the names they called her. Last week she'd been on a bus, and now she had a car worth more than their families brought home in a year. All because a well-dressed man had shown up on the street a few times. Her eyes stung with tears, but she wouldn't let them fall.

Those boys had a point. In a way, she had traded her body for the car. Bile burned the back of her throat as she drove to the Carlton House to drop off Cash and pick up Evie. If strangers could see what she'd done, would she be able to hide it from those who had known her best?

Chapter Six

Brandon felt the electricity in the air even before he saw Megan. He tried to listen to whatever it was Gemma found so important, but her words passed through his brain as he scanned the crowd filling the ballroom of the Beverly Carlton. His gaze found Megan like a heat-seeking missile, though she had her back to him and seemed caught up in the tangle of people surrounding her.

There was something about the way she held her shoulders, something that wasn't quite right. He'd always kept his distance from her at events, keeping up the veil of privacy they lived their relationship under, so he was very accustomed to watching her. And she was not herself.

"What are you looking at?" Gemma laid her hand on his arm and leaned into him.

In that brief moment, Megan turned and registered his presence. Or he thought she had, but she seemed to be looking down and to the left, her expression laced with poison. Brandon followed her dagger-filled gaze straight to Gemma.

He looked back to Megan, annoyance filling him. Megan could not possibly think anything was going on with Gemma. It was utterly ridiculous, and more than a little insulting.

He'd never given Megan any reason not to trust him. Gemma was his oldest friend, another lonely only child from the estate neighboring his parents. She was a sister, a fact that was awkwardly apparent the one and only time she'd kissed him. Something clicked in his mind, like the ignition on a gas stove, but nothing sparked.

"Megan Carlton?" Gemma straightened back up. "Your mother told her she needs to make an appearance at all the major events to build her reputation back up. If she wasn't such a bitch, I'd feel bad for her, having to answer all the questions everyone must have about her father."

"Megan's reputation is impeccable. It's her father who's got problems."

"Megan is a Carlton asking for money. I don't think anyone will be signing up to give her more after how her father swindled so many people. Including you. Have you managed to find him yet?"

"Your fiancé is working on that."

Gemma cringed. "Don't call him that. He's probably only doing it to drive me insane, but I don't see what other choice I have since you have your mystery woman."

"Danny is good people, Gemma." Brandon watched as two of the more vapid guys from their social set crowded Megan. The type of boys who never grew up and only cared about how quickly they could spend their family money, Brandon had little patience for them. More so when one rubbed Megan's arm and didn't let go as she tried to pull away.

"Daniel gets some sick delight out of teasing me. He always has, since that first time you brought him home with you from school." Gemma kept talking, but Brandon had stopped listening completely.

He crossed the room without knowing he meant to, his feet carrying him without thought. He didn't need to hear the words being thrown at Megan by the crowd around her, their ugliness reflected on the faces of the people she used to consider friends. Some friends.

"Excuse me," he said, stepping between Megan and the worthless troll who hadn't had the manners to let go of her arm.

He tried to steer her away, but a voice behind him stopped him cold. "You should wait your turn."

Brandon turned and took two steps towards the coward who thought it a good idea to torment a woman. His woman. "What did you say?"

The idiot's chin quivered, as it should. Taking out the frustrations of the last few months on this fool would be welcome. He could take this troll outside and show everyone that if they messed with Megan, he would lay them out one by one.

Megan's hand wrapped around his clenched fist. "Brandon, please. Not now."

He twined her fingers in his and lifted his chin at the worm. There was more than one way to hurt someone. If he couldn't do it physically, he'd make sure the Patrick clan found their way into some financial trouble.

He turned and led Megan from the ballroom, grateful that she didn't try and pry their hands apart even though their exit turned more than a few heads. He pulled her through the hallway and into one of the empty conference rooms the organizers of the party had used to hold decorations before the event. He closed the door and pulled her to him, half-expecting her to push him away.

Whatever had been said in that room had cut her deeper than he feared because she clung to him as if he were her ballast, and he held her closer. She wrapped her arms around his waist, her hands under the jacket of his dark suit and her head tucked beneath his chin.

He felt her shaky breaths as she calmed herself, and he cursed every one of the spoiled grown-children who'd made her feel less than she was. No wonder she'd run to Pasadena. She must have guessed the jackals would turn on her if she'd stayed.

Megan breathed in the familiar scent of Brandon's cologne and listened to the sound of his steady heartbeat beneath her ear until she no longer wanted to cry. She'd known facing everyone again wouldn't be pretty, but she'd never imagined it would get quite that ugly. She held tighter to Brandon, trying to absorb his strength and stability. She needed enough of it to shore her up for a while, like for the rest of her life.

As she calmed down, she realized even Brandon must have an agenda. Yes, he felt guilty about what had happened to her family at his own hand, but there was more to it. He wanted to have his cake and eat it too, and there was one particular slice of devil's food in the ballroom that was going to be none too happy about the way he'd left the scene.

That wasn't her problem. Right now she just needed a booster shot of the confidence she used to have to immunize her against the next few weeks. People were angry about the money they lost because of her father and she was the only Carlton left for them to take their frustrations out on. Knowing that didn't make the snide remarks and licentious comments any easier to take.

"Hey, you okay?" Brandon leaned back and lifted her chin with his finger. She looked up and wondered how she was supposed to replace such a satin-voiced, dark chocolate-eyed, scrumptious-smelling man. He'd ruined her in so many ways, financially didn't even register.

She nodded like a bobble head, still unsure if she could

talk without breaking. Instead she melted into his chocolate gaze like an ice-cream cone in August, and felt her cheeks lift in a smile in spite of her attempts to remain immune. He'd come through when she needed a friend the most, and she couldn't help but be grateful.

"I don't believe you, but I think everyone else will." He released her and stepped back, forcing her to reluctantly give up her hold on him or look like a clingy fool. "You look beautiful."

"Thank you," she whispered automatically, lifting a hand to her hair. She knew twirling a curl in her fingers made her look nervous, but she couldn't help herself.

"I thought you said you would never wear this dress again."

She blinked, remembering how the zipper had gotten stuck when she'd tried to release it. Six months ago it had fit like a sausage casing, now it looked as good on as she'd imagined it would when she'd bought it. The memory made her brighten enough to smile up at him.

"I've learned to never say never."

A cocksure grin lit his face and he took her hand. "I'm glad to hear that."

Before she could explain that she was still firm on never having sex with him again, he opened the door and started walking back towards the hallway to the ballroom, pulling her along with him.

"Wait a minute."

"Nope, not a minute to lose. You came to work the party, not get attacked by the petulant offspring of the people you need to solicit donations from. We need to get you swirling in the right crowd."

He kept up his pace, oblivious that she had to take two

steps to his one, in three-inch heels no less. "Brandon, slow down. We can't go back in there together."

"We can and we are. I told you I'm done hiding out."

She pulled her hand free of his, nearly stumbling from the loss of his momentum. "We're not together anymore, so there is nothing to keep private. And if I let you lead me into that room, I can forget about clawing back the respect I'll need to be an effective fundraiser."

He turned to face her, the little crease between his eyes deepening. "If I show that I trust you after the Carlton Hotels deal, then everyone will see that they can trust you too."

"You actually believe that." Megan shook her head. "There are plenty of people who'll see us together and think that I came with everything else you bought."

His eyes widened in shock. "That's not my fault."

"Nothing ever is." She found herself standing taller, more centered than she'd been before his rescue. Maybe his confidence was as infectious as his cologne.

"We're not discussing this here. But if we'd been open with everyone from the start—"

"You didn't want that."

She softened her gaze, trying to explain. "Don't you see? If you parade me in there like a trophy, they'll be right."

"You've got to be kidding."

"You'll expect me to go home with you in exchange." She shrugged and swallowed over the ache in her throat. "And everyone will think I went along with it because of all the money my father owes you. You know what that would make me."

He blinked slowly and took a step closer. "I don't like where this train of thought is headed. I have wanted to be with you, to take care of you, since long before you needed me to."

"What I need is to do this on my own. I have to know that I can take care of myself."

He nodded. "Fair enough, but that doesn't mean I have to pretend you don't exist."

When he offered her his arm, she took it, knowing that fighting with him would be pointless. Heads did turn as they reentered the fray, but instead of the swarm of prying scandalmongers she'd had to face when she arrived, this time she was led straight to his mother.

Jordana Knight welcomed her with a kiss on the cheek and then piloted her about the room as she greeted cautious former friends of her family. Brandon didn't hover, but he didn't disappear into the woodwork either. Every time she felt the slightest unease, her gaze found him within seconds, as if they were bound together by an unseen tether, and her anxiety melted in the assurance of his smile.

She looked to him each time someone saw fit to confide in her how they'd questioned her father's business decisions or her mother's parenting choices over the years. A few of them seemed to be almost apologizing for not speaking up when her father had started collecting for his express hotel expansion or when her mother had allowed her and her sisters to do crazy things like head to Mardi Gras unsupervised.

The trouble with being a teenager was that you only thought to push the boundaries, and when you had none, there was no telling what you could get away with. She didn't think her parents were so lenient because of a lack of affection, just of responsibility. They'd wanted babies, and had no idea what to do with children once they were too old for a nanny.

She knew neither of them were going to win a parenting award, but it was still hard to hear them criticized so harshly. After all, the results of their efforts weren't so bad. Ava was starting her own business, the scandal had barely registered with Briana who had returned to college as if nothing had changed in her world, and then there was the woman facing them.

As apprehensive as Megan was about her abilities and reputation, she was proud of standing her ground and sticking to what she believed in. Though the boys at the car today had thought she was a whore, and a few permanently adolescent heirs to family money thought she should be to make up for their financial losses, she hadn't actually slipped beneath the moral code she'd set for herself as a teen.

Her stomach clenched, thinking of how she'd taken the car from Malibu. Brandon would have to take it back tonight, just as she was taking back her life. If he wanted to be friends without benefits, she would stay open to that. For so long he was her best friend, and she didn't want to throw that away as easily as he had.

Her whole life things had come easy to her. Family money opened many doors and provided the security to do as you pleased. When her parents had disappeared with her trust fund and she'd discovered that Brandon had taken up with Gemma, the rug had been pulled out from under her and she'd fallen.

Hard.

But she was getting up. The scrapes were healing, and there would be scars left behind so that she would never forget how quickly security could fall away and leave her with only herself to depend on.

She tacked on a smile as the elderly Raleigh sisters commiserated about how sad it was that her parents hadn't thought to take their daughters with them when they fled the country. It seemed in every conversation she had to bring it back around to the Carlton Houses and how important it was that she was still here to help with such a worthy endeavor.

As they nodded their agreement, Megan looked up and found Brandon without searching. Her smile went from fake to genuine. He might not be the man she'd share the rest of her life with, but they had shared some wonderful moments.

Just as she couldn't let the current scandal change her opinion of her mother, she wouldn't let Brandon's current indiscretions change what she'd thought of him. He'd been wonderful to her, her first love, her first lover, her first heartbreak.

Her shredded heart tightened in her chest at the realization that they were truly over. She hoped now they could be friends, and that he would learn to accept that they would never again be more.

"This is ridiculous, Megan." Brandon waited for her to buckle into the passenger seat of her car before he started it up and headed for her dreadful idea of an apartment. "The Bentley is yours."

"It belonged to Carlton International. I'll get a car eventually." She folded her hands on her lap as prim as if she were one of the nuns at the parochial school he'd attended.

"Why do you insist on doing everything the hard way?"

"Just because I don't want to do things your way, doesn't mean it's the hard way."

"You'd be doing me a favor if you let me help you. I go crazy thinking of all the things that can go wrong with this little independence plan of yours."

She huffed a breath and stared out the window. Brandon gripped the steering wheel, wishing for all he was worth that she weren't so damned stubborn. A woman who knew her own mind was attractive in most circumstances, but this was maddening.

"How are you going to get Cash if you don't have a car?"

"I'll pick him up after my shift at the coffee shop and we'll walk. It's good exercise."

"You have to work tomorrow?"

"Today, technically." She tapped the clock on the dash. "In three hours."

"That's insane."

Megan shrugged. "It doesn't usually feel early because I'm getting off my shift at the bar."

"And how do you plan on getting to work without a car?"

"The same way I have for the two months before you tried to ride in on your white horse. I'll take the bus." When she pushed her hair behind her ears he noticed a slight shake to her hand.

"It would be safer if you would use the car."

"I am safer in that neighborhood than the car is."

"Yes, but I can replace it."

The silence hung heavy between them as he navigated the freeways, still sprinkled with traffic even at the late hour. He'd agreed to take her home only after she'd threatened to leave the car at the hotel and take the bus.

He'd hoped to use the drive from Beverly Hills to Pasadena to talk her into coming home with him, but she wasn't playing into his hand. Hadn't since he'd led her back into the ballroom.

Maybe he shouldn't have tried to build her confidence back up. If he'd led her out of the hotel before she'd had time to rally, she probably would have given in and given up on this plan to make it completely on her own.

"You know, Meg, everyone needs help now and again. You can't live in a bubble."

"I know. My bubble burst." She gave a sad laugh at her attempt at a joke. "I can take care of myself, maybe not to the level at which I was raised, but most people don't live like that. Most people live like I do, worrying about the rent and having to wear the same old dress to parties."

"Your life is not a social experiment. I have complete confidence that you can continue on like this indefinitely. I also know you well enough to know that you're miserable like this. Life's too short to waste simply proving a point."

"I won't do this forever. I miss my sisters." She drew in a deep breath that tugged at an emptiness deep in his soul. The sigh that followed was long, and sounded too much like defeat. "After the funding is secure for the houses, I think I'll head to Oregon to see Briana."

"You're going to run even farther away? You think that will help?" His ears prickled as red-hot rage flashed through him. She wasn't just running away from the scandal, she was running away from him.

"She really seems to like it there, and she swears it doesn't rain half as much as people think."

"Is this the part where I beg you not to go?" He couldn't keep the bitterness from his tone.

"I hope not. It would help more if you told me to have a nice life." She swiped at her cheek and he resisted the urge to pull the car over.

"Your life won't be nice without me in it."

"That's a bit egocentric, even for you."

"When are you going to stop punishing me for something that isn't even my fault?"

"Probably about the time you realize that what happened was completely of your own making."

"I suppose you think I should have let some stranger come in and take the hotels? If it wasn't me, it would have been someone else, and they wouldn't have cared enough to keep the original hotels together. Your family history has always meant so much to you. I thought you might want them." He turned down her street, the flashing lights atop police cars making him squint. He banged his hand on the steering wheel. "Do you see? You are not safe here."

"As if there have never been a few police cars outside your parents' estate. I'm sure they're just here breaking up some party."

"In this neighborhood I doubt the police have time to bother with noise ordinances." He pulled along the curb behind one of the patrol cars and killed the engine. He turned towards her to explain that under no circumstances could he allow her to stay here, but before he got a word out one of the bodyguards knocked on her window.

Megan screamed and nearly jumped out of her skin, proving to him that no matter her bravado, she was not prepared for this.

"Hey," he said, taking her hands in his. "It's okay. I want you to stay in the car while I find out what's going on."

Her thin brows knit together when he climbed out of the car, but she didn't follow, so at least she'd heard that much. He stepped up on the curb, nodding at the men he'd interviewed personally.

"Any idea what happened?" Brandon asked, glancing back at the car. Megan sat stark still, staring straight ahead.

"Break in, about two hours ago," the younger of the two men spoke in low tones, barely above a whisper. "It took the

103

police over an hour to respond."

His throat tightened. "Was it—"

The older man nodded, cutting off the question. "Six boys who'll have to spend some time in the adult system. Word is they got bored while waiting for her to come home and did quite the number on the apartment."

A kind of fear he'd never imagine possible washed over him, spiking his bloodstream with adrenaline and ice. He stared up at the windows of her apartment, watching shadows move behind the curtains. His mind started to play snippets of scenes of what might have been, and he struggled to stop them all. His stomach twisted in a series of knots that would have held a fifty-foot sloop.

"I called it in and waited. I would have stopped her if she'd come home alone." The younger man's words drifted in, but Brandon could only register them with a nod.

A hollow banging rang out and he looked up to see a uniformed officer shouldering a pimpled teen down the cement stairs on the side of the building. The handcuffed kid's baggy jeans and over-sized shoes seemed to be tripping him up. If it weren't so terrifying, it might be comical.

Brandon heard his own breath grow louder as he stared at the teen, his muscles twitching as they primed for a fight that he knew would never be. Still, his body responded, ready to squeeze the life from this bastard as surely as it would have been snuffed out of Megan.

He watched as the teen wriggled against his captor, nearly falling over the final stair. The cop jerked the kid's head up and recognition registered on the scum's ugly face as his gaze fell on the car with Megan alone inside. Brandon twitched, barely managing to rein in his need to put himself between Megan and danger. She was safe in the car and if he did anything to let on what had happened, she might try to get out.

Rapid-fire Spanish flew from the bastard's mouth, his tone taunting and nasty. Brandon's brain translated immediately, as if the words had been flung in English. He didn't know he'd lunged until the younger bodyguard blocked his way, the older man's arm firm across his chest.

"That garbage isn't worth it." The older man spoke, but seemed to know better than to release his hold until the patrol car door slammed.

Megan clutched Cash to her chest, her breath still unsteady. The hard glint in Brandon's dark eyes haunted her from the mirrored walls of the elevator. He'd barely spoken to her in the last few hours, nothing outside of one-word answers she wouldn't have disagreed with even if she wanted to. Right now, he was not a man to be crossed.

And she wasn't in any condition to fight. The aftershocks of seeing what they'd done to her apartment still echoed in her mind. There was no telling what they would have done to Cash if he'd been there, to her if she'd come home alone.

It was all a tangled mess of things she didn't want to ever have to comb through. If only she could shave it from her mind completely.

It would be hard to forget the words they'd written on the walls, how they'd torn every piece of clothing she owned, or her irrational anger at the mess they'd made on her great-grandmother's quilt. She'd always remember the way Brandon had stood beside her, lending her his silent strength when hers had depleted. He'd even shaken off the quilt and put it in a garbage bag, giving it to the front desk with the directions to have it cleaned and repaired.

Funny, she'd toiled for weeks to earn enough money for the

charging pad for the phone, but she'd been cut low by the desecration of the one thing she'd brought with her. As the elevator doors parted, she had the strange realization that though she and Brandon had been together in his penthouse countless times, they'd never ridden up in the elevator together. They'd always kept up the pretence and gone up separately.

She followed him into the small foyer, the door to his penthouse on the right, what had been her father's on the left. No one had once questioned why she frequented the hotel, always assuming she used the penthouse after a night of partying rather than returning home. They were right, just not about which penthouse.

Brandon held open the door for her and she walked into the place she'd spent more nights than not before her world tilted and she slid into oblivion. Hearing the door close, the slide of the deadbolt, the beep of the alarm, Brandon's footfalls as he retreated to the bedroom, all of it served to relax her shoulders and lower her guard. In spite of the events of the night, she hadn't felt this safe in months.

Cash wriggled from her arms, his nails clicking on the marble tiles on the entryway before being silenced by the thick rugs on the dark wood floors as he scampered into the kitchen. She wondered if he'd be disappointed not to find his water dish in the butler's pantry, but when she heard his faint slurping her heart tumbled. For better or worse, they were as close to home as they got.

Brandon emerged from the bedroom wearing only a pair of black lounge pants slung low on his hips. She couldn't help but notice the hard ridges of his abdomen and the smooth planes of his muscled chest. She looked for the evidence she'd left on his body, but didn't see the slightest trace.

He crossed the room to the wet bar and poured himself

more bourbon than she'd ever seen him drink. He didn't like to drink, didn't like to blur the edges or lose control. He tossed it back with barely a wince and poured another.

"You need to give it a minute and let it kick in." She ran her palms along the rough lace of her skirt, unsure of what to do with her hands.

"I don't think I have enough for it to even make a dent." He swallowed another glassful, banging it on the marble countertop.

"Unless you've started drinking, it shouldn't take long for things to get fuzzy."

"Promise?" He poured another.

"Seriously, give it some time."

"Go to bed, Megan." He swirled the glass, never once looking up at her as he walked to the wall of windows and stared out at the twinkling lights of the city.

She twisted her hands in front of her. "I'm going to need to borrow a T-shirt to wear since I don't have anything." Her voice cracked, but she swallowed and continued. "And I'll sleep in the guest room."

"Whatever you want, Megan. Your closet is nearly full, but go ahead and take whatever you want."

The urge to go to him and wrap her arms around him and apologize for how he felt was strong, but she didn't give in. She was as shaken by the events of the night as he was, which didn't leave her in a place to comfort someone else, and so she retreated.

She'd rarely been in the guest bedroom of the penthouse, always staking her claim on the king bed and the man who slept in it. The guest room was decorated like the rest of the hotel, understated with light colors and rich fabrics. She sat on the bench at the end of the canopy bed and slid off her heels, rubbing at the soles of her feet.

Fear and exhaustion combined to make her both wired and tired. Maybe Brandon's idea of drinking into a stupor had some merit. She got up and opened the door of the walk-in closet, turning on the light as she stepped inside. Confusion flooded her as she looked around at more clothes than she'd seen since she'd left her parents estate.

Looking closer, she tried to place when and where she'd worn things last. These weren't the things she'd left at her parents or things she'd sold at the consignment shop, but clothes she must have left here over the years. There were shelves of sweaters, which made sense because they were always the first to come off and she doubted she ever took the time to look for them when she left. Jeans, dresses, shoes, evening bags by the dozen.

Had she really been so disconnected that she hadn't realized just how much was here? She usually came with a bag, but it was obvious she'd rarely left with one.

She turned to her left and her heart stuttered. Her entire lingerie collection hung neatly on padded hangers, carefully finger-spaced apart. Maybe she'd never noticed the things she left behind because everything must have been tucked into his closet like her lingerie had been.

At least he'd had the decency to transfer her things before he moved Gemma in. Since so much remained, Gemma probably had no idea what he kept hidden in the guest room. If she'd found such a stash she would have burned every piece.

Thoughts of Brandon's new lover did serve to push down the events of the night. Megan rubbed her face, knowing that staying here was only a temporary option. She couldn't stomach having to see Gemma and Brandon play house.

She reached out and fingered the soft silk of one of her nightgowns. None of them were entirely appropriate for sleeping. Lingerie had been more playwear than anything else. Brandon had a thing for red. And sheer. And lace. And flyaway baby dolls that would release with a quick tug on the ribbons holding them closed. Some of it was playful like the Santa teddy. Some had made her feel so incredibly sexy.

She found an aubergine nightgown with a slit so high even her legs seemed long in it. The lace along the halter neckline seemed to push things together and used to make her feel like a siren. She lifted the hanger and carried it into the ensuite bathroom and hung it on the back of the door. She turned the steam shower on full before stripping out of her dress and underwear.

Beneath the spray, she tried to scrub off the events of the day, of the last few months. Maybe if she scrubbed hard enough she'd get back to who she used to be, how she used to feel. Steam billowed around her, curling her hair and relaxing her muscles. She let the water course over her body until her limbs felt week and heavy.

As she dried off, she wondered if she might be able to make it to bed before the sensation evaporated like the steam. She finger-combed her hair and toweled it dry before slipping the nightgown over her head. The silk whispered against her skin, the lace of the bodice molding to her curves.

The cool air prickled her skin as she left the bathroom in search of Cash. The penthouse was dark, only the faint moonlight illuminating the rooms. Megan knew every inch as if it were her own home, but that didn't make finding a tiny black dog in the dark any easier.

Everything was still, and she didn't want to wake Brandon in case his bourbon binge had led him to sleep. After a few

Chapter Seven

Brandon leaned back against the padded headboard and watched Megan patter about the darkened living room. He crossed his legs at the ankles and enjoyed the view as she searched the place for something while wearing the sexiest nightgown she owned—and given her collection that was saying something.

With the French doors of his bedroom open, he could clearly see her as she rummaged around, but he couldn't think of what she might be looking for. He was nearly past the point of thinking at all. A few more drinks and he might actually be able to sleep. Megan was right in that he hadn't been much of a drinker before she left, but since she'd been gone he'd taken to having a glass or two each night as he stared at a door that never opened.

It used to be that he never knew when she'd show up. Sometimes he'd come home to find her playing show tunes on the piano in the living room, other times she'd bound in tipsy from a party and demand a proper nightcap. He liked it best when she'd wake him out of a sound sleep with her mouth. It was almost worth falling asleep just for the possibility. But given the state of things between them, the probability was nil.

She moved to his doorway, peeking in as if she didn't belong. Brandon blinked to make sure he wasn't imagining it, and then realized that she couldn't see him. He'd drawn the drapes, so his room wasn't showered in moonlight the way the rest of the penthouse was. She took a tentative step inside and his cheeks tightened in a smile.

"Too scared to sleep?" he asked, setting his half-full glass on the nightstand.

She jumped at the sound of his voice, placing a hand on the exposed skin of her chest before she turned towards the bed. "I didn't know you were up."

He wanted to make a comment about her nightgown causing his current state, but couldn't. In the dark she didn't know, and they weren't in that place anymore.

She cleared her throat and looked around again. "Is Cash in here?"

"He's asleep in the loft. His bed is next to Money's." When she turned, he could no longer see her face, just the shadowed curve of her body. Somehow he'd escaped hell, only to land in purgatory.

He caught the smile on her face as she turned. "You have his bed? I thought it must still be at Kimberly's."

"Oh, it probably is. I got a smaller version of the one I have for Money. He seemed to like it."

She inched closer to the bed and it took everything in him not to grab her, pull her to him and convince her of where she needed to be. "Thank you for taking him in. I don't know what I would have done if I'd lost him."

"Yeah, I know the feeling." His throat tightened with emotions he didn't want to feel and words he couldn't say. He couldn't tell her he was angry at the way she'd abandoned Cash, couldn't tell her he was hurt at how she'd left him as if he were nothing, couldn't even tell her how stupid she'd been about where she'd chosen to live. He couldn't say a thing, because if he did, she'd walk right back into harm's way.

"Where is Money?" She stepped closer to the end of the bed, the slight shift from one foot to the other telling her nervousness.

"Malibu." He tilted his head, wishing he could see more than her outline. His Megan had only been nervous a handful of times in her life, always barreling through life with confidence in spades. This creature radiated anxiety, not that he could blame her after the events of the night.

"You don't keep him with you?"

"I was gone this week, so he stayed with the dog walker down there. Once it's light out I'll go get him."

"Oh, okay. I'll let you get some sleep." She turned to go.

"I'm not going to sleep, Megan."

She turned back towards the bed. "We could play backgammon if you want. I'll even let you win."

"I don't want to play games anymore." His voice thickened as his throat grew tight. "Come here."

"I don't want—"

"Yes, you do."

She hesitated only slightly before coming around to her side of the bed and pulling back the sheets. She climbed on and slid her feet beneath the covers as she scooted towards the middle. He pulled her to him, his body finally beginning to uncoil as he held her close. The terror of the night had wound him so tight, he'd wondered if he'd ever relax again.

Her hair was slightly damp beneath his chin, her feet cold against his leg, but the reality of having her home and safe warmed his soul. He laid his cheek against her head and played with the strands of her hair.

"I've missed you," he whispered in spite of himself.

He felt her nod as her arms wound around him. "I miss me too."

He smiled until he felt her shudder against him, a warm wetness against his bare chest. "Hey now, you're safe."

"They ruined everything I had left." She choked out the words around sobs, the sound so pitiful it softened his anger.

"You're safe. That's all that matters."

"I don't know why they would do something like that. I never did anything to them, and now I have nothing. Not a single thing."

"You have Cash." He massaged her scalp, choosing his words carefully. "You can have me."

She gasped, then let out a slow breath. The deep breaths that followed as she calmed herself lasted for long moments where he mentally kicked himself for pushing. He wanted to convince her that he knew what was best for the both of them, but he couldn't risk pushing her away.

"I don't want you to go back there."

"Me either." She shifted against him, lifting her hand to wipe her eyes.

"I want you to stay here." The statement hung heavy in the air.

"I don't know if I can do that. I need to work and—"

"So work for me." She stiffened in his arms so he talked faster. "You could take care of Money for me and go to school, or you could get a job at the hotel. That's why you got your GED, right? So you could do something other than serve people drinks?"

"Yes, but I can't depend on you for everything. I owe you too much already and I have no way to ever pay you back. The only thing I have that you want, it makes me, it's just..." Her chest rose and fell with her heaving breaths as she struggled for words.

"Were you with me for the last seven years because of my money?"

"Don't be ridiculous. I never even thought about it. But now—"

"Now you need to realize that I'm not going to have any less money and you're not going to be any less sexy. It is what it is, Megan. It hasn't mattered for the last seven years and it doesn't matter now."

"It's not that simple."

"It's not that complicated. Either you want to be with me or you don't. Our bank balances never had a place in it before, and they don't now."

"That's easy for you to say. You have everything. You're the one with all the control. I have nothing to offer and so it's like putting a price on my soul."

"For the last seven years you've dictated when and where we'd be together. You had all the control. For a long time I thought it was the ideal arrangement because I didn't have to share you. When we were together, there was never anyone else around, no distractions, no competing for your attention. But when I wanted more, wanted you to move in here and stop sneaking around, you played it off like a joke. For God's sake Meg, I asked you to marry me."

"That didn't count." She shifted against him, but he held her closer, not wanting her to get away before he had an answer one way or the other.

"It counted for me."

"Brandon, we were together when you asked me."

"Of course we were together."

"No, I mean, you were inside of me every time you brought it up. I can't take you seriously if you only mention it during sex."

He couldn't help the laugh, and he couldn't stop it even when she punched him in the shoulder. He'd always assumed that was romantic, that one day someone would ask her how he proposed and she'd give him a knowing look and they'd get back home as soon as possible. "When was I supposed to ask you? We didn't go anywhere together except the Malibu house, and whenever we were together the odds were that we were making love. We're very good at it, remember?"

He pressed his lips to her temple, peppering tiny kisses down the side of her face. She lifted her head and he leaned in to kiss her, but she stopped him with a finger against his lips.

"Brandon, why is it sex is all people see in me?" Her raw whisper tore through his heart. "It's always been that way, and I never understood it, so it scared me. But tonight with the guys at the party and then the gang at the apartment, it all crashed down."

He framed her face in his hands, smoothing the wetness on her cheeks with his thumbs. "It wasn't you they saw, baby. They saw vulnerability and opportunity and wanted to take advantage of both. They didn't see you holding your head high in a room full of people who would have rather written you off than faced their own mistakes. They didn't see your determination to make something of yourself on your own terms, or how you've shouldered the responsibilities of an entire family on your own. They didn't see all you've accomplished. They only tried to find where you were exposed and exploit it. They didn't see you at all."

"Thank you." She pulled in a shaky breath. "But isn't that what you're doing? Taking me in at a weak moment and expecting some payoff? It's not as ugly on the outside, but it's not as pretty as your words either. We've only been here a few hours, and yet we've fallen back into bed as if the last few months never happened."

He shook his head, for the first time seeing it from her side and cringing because she had a point. "We'll always wind up back here, no matter what happens. It's where we belong, Megan. I'm not going to lie and say that I don't want you, but I'll be fine as long as I know you'll be sleeping beside me at night. It can be just that simple until you're ready for more. As long as you agree to stay here, I won't push for anything else."

She turned her face into his hand and kissed his palm. "It's hard to believe you after what's happened, especially when I know you can convince anyone to see things your way."

"You don't want to hear my reasons for doing what I did, so all I can do now is show you that you're first with me. I don't care how long it takes for us to get back on track, as long as that is where we're heading."

"But what if we don't work anymore? I'm different now. I don't even feel like myself most of the time."

"You've been a fish out of water, and until you find what you want to do, you will be for a while longer. But we can either grow together or grow apart. Because even if you think you've changed, there is a part of you that is still that sassy, sexy Megan Carlton I fell for, and I don't want to risk losing her ever again."

"Good." Beneath his hands, he felt her cheeks lift in a smile he couldn't see in the dark. She turned away, settling herself beneath the covers and lying back against the pillows.

Brandon sat still for long moments, trying to decide if he really could do it, really could simply sleep next to her and not try for more. He probably would reach for her in his sleep just out of habit, and then she'd never believe he hadn't planned it.

Her hand reached out and rested on his thigh, his pulse spiking at the contact. Maybe she meant to torture him with teasing touches for the next few days. That was fine. He'd give her a couple of days to settle in and then seduce her properly.

"Brandon?"

"Yeah?" His pulse ticked higher at the sound of her voice. He pushed a hand through his hair and wished a certain part of his body didn't respond so enthusiastically to such little encouragement.

"I can't sleep." Her fingers curled around his leg and all he could see in his mind was the last time they curled around his cock, and he was really starting to wish he hadn't gone for the last drink because reining in his desire was as hard as he was right now.

"Just try." His voice sounded like it had been dragged over gravel.

"I think it's that I don't feel like me. Before I always thought it was because I was so out of my comfort zone, but I've always been comfortable here."

"You will be again." He covered her hand with his and lifted it to his mouth for a quick kiss. He laid their hands on the bed between them, not trusting the temptation of her hand anywhere on his body.

They'd never been very good at this part, the companionable silences and chaste moments. Keeping their relationship private meant they never got to be together as much as he would have liked, so every instance felt like making up for lost time. He tried to think of the last time they'd shared a bed without making love, and he only came up with lurid moments of falling into bed in a post-coital haze.

He sat up straighter, trying to ease the throbbing ache in

his groin. His mind might be having an easier time with her safely ensconced in his bed, but his dick was not interested in the intellectual reasons why it would be stuck behind pants for the foreseeable future.

All the experiences of his misspent youth had taught him to live in the now and take advantage of opportunities as they presented themselves. Not for the first time, he was glad he'd been wild enough to warrant a stint in military school. That training was the only thing keeping him on his side of the bed.

"Can I tell you a secret?" she whispered like a schoolgirl.

"Sure." He swallowed, trying to decide if finishing his drink would help or harm his current situation.

"I miss sex." She let out a sigh that sent what little blood was left in his brain south. "The excitement and the pleasure and the absolute freedom of it. I hadn't thought much about it lately, but as I'm lying here it's all I can think about."

"Let me know if there is anything you need my help with."

"I always figured I was a pretty sexual person," she said as if she hadn't heard his offer. "But that part of me kind of shut down. Maybe it's just the availability that gets me going."

He cleared his throat. "Megan, I said I'd wait and I'm trying to mean it. But you have to cut me a break here. I haven't had sex since August twentieth, so I need you to either go to sleep or talk about something else."

"August twentieth, huh?" He felt the bed dip as she propped herself up on her elbow.

"I may have looked it up a few times."

"Maybe that's my problem. I've hit some kind of three-month alarm."

"The only alarm that should be going off is the one that tells you to stop teasing me unless you actually want me to make love to you until you're so exhausted you can't even lift your head."

Her laugh was a wicked temptation, and completely Megan. "You've only managed that twice, but I should leave that as an open invitation. I'd have to turn in my credentials as a woman if I didn't encourage that kind of attention at any opportunity."

"Babe, this is your last warning. Stop now or I won't be able to until one of us passes out."

"Really?" She sat up and he wished he could have seen her as she pulled her nightgown over her head and tossed it to the floor. Before he could reach for her, she'd straddled him, her hands wrapped around his biceps to keep his arms still. She leaned forward just enough to dart out her tongue and lick the seam of his lips. "My bet is that you go first."

"I'm just as sure that you'll come first." He leaned in to fulfill the promise of the kiss, but she leaned back.

"You did buy condoms, right?"

Reality flickered into his mind just long enough for him to remember the strategic locations he'd placed them throughout the penthouse. "So many I think the clerk thought I was heading to an orgy."

The naughty laugh was back, and so was his Megan. She met his kiss with a playful passion of her own. The only thing missing from the moment was light so he could see her bare body. Though, given his current state of near-painful arousal, the visual of her naked might send him over the edge.

He lifted his hands, loving the way her fingers curled around his biceps as he cupped her breasts. He squeezed her, remembering the weight and textures before he rolled her nipples between his fingers. She moaned in pleasure and covered his hands with hers.

She started to rock her pelvis against his erection, so he

slipped a hand between them and palmed her. The silky, slippery softness of her made him groan. He'd wanted to make sure she came before he even got the condom opened, but it was next to impossible not to flip her to her back and bury himself inside of her.

Megan's lips trailed over his jaw and down his throat, her voice weaving through the erotic haze. "Where?"

"What?" He tried to think, but couldn't get beyond how amazing she felt, so soft and smooth and the head of her clit seemed longer and thicker than usual.

Her legs started to tremble and her fingernails dug into his shoulders as she cried out in pleasure. She leaned forward, pressing the heel of his palm against her clit as she rode out the waves of her orgasm. Brandon tried to feel the relief of knowing she'd gone first, but couldn't get beyond his own need and how amazingly sexy she felt against his skin.

She hummed and licked his earlobe and his body twitched in response. "Find a condom now, or else."

"Or else what?" He reached to the nightstand, pulling open the drawer and finding the box inside.

"Or else I use you like a toy and you get nothing." She lifted herself off him and roughly pushed her hands into the waistband of his lounge pants, shoving them down over his hips. He tilted his hips to help her, rewarding her with a condom packet and a smile when she straddled him again. But she couldn't see either because she wrapped both hands around his engorged cock and squeezed.

He cursed, then grabbed one of her wrists. "Put the condom on."

He heard her hair swish against her shoulders as she must have shaken her head. "It's dark and I don't want to do it wrong."

"You won't."

"Seriously, I don't have much practice. I'd need to see you and I like the dark." She leaned forward and licked his earlobe again, making his entire body as tight as a fist. "It's like we're both blindfolded."

Oh, she was wicked. He sheathed himself quickly. Megan wasted no time guiding him into position. She wrapped her hand around his girth, rubbing him along her slick folds.

"I thought you said if I got a condom you wouldn't use me as a toy." He clenched his teeth and wrapped his hands around her hips.

"You like it." She lifted and then lowered her body, sliding his cock home in one sure movement.

Her tight heat clutched him, pleasure rocketing through his body. His hands slid around to her butt, squeezing the firm globes as she rocked against him, her breaths already starting to come fast and shallow. He helped her tip forward, knowing it gave her clit direct contact.

She reached for the headboard as she rolled her hips, holding him within her as she took her pleasure. He reached up and threaded his hand through her hair, pulling her mouth to his.

He'd kissed her too many times to keep score, but this held the excitement of the first and the passion of the moment and the experience of knowing exactly what she liked. A deluge of need saturated his mind, and he knew he needed more than her deliberate rocking. He wanted to dive into her, again and again, and that wasn't going to happen until Megan found her next orgasm.

With one hand still in her hair, he moved the other one to her breast, giving it a gentle squeeze before he began flicking his thumbnail over her nipple. She turned her head away from his kiss and rested her forehead on his shoulder while she ground harder against him.

"Can't breathe," she whispered, but didn't change her pace. He heard her breathing begin to stagger and knew she was close. He wet his thumbs and brushed them against her nipples. She cried out his name, tossing her head back as she took the final strokes towards her bliss.

Her orgasm caught him in a vise, nearly pitching him over the edge with her. He wanted to, needed to find his release like he needed his next breath, but it was just out of reach. While he still felt the tiny quakes of her inner muscles, he rolled her to her back, still deep within her. He slid his hand beneath her knee, pushing it back until he could lever her leg on his shoulder.

He slowly thrust forward, filling her to the hilt. He groaned in pleasure, then began the steady rhythm of sinking and rising. Megan's soft pants turned into pleas of encouragement, her hair rasping against the mattress as she turned her head from side to side. He knew just what she looked like, her golden hair spread out on the mattress like a naughty halo, her hands squeezing her breasts and her fingers plucking at her nipples until they stood out taut and tender, her big blue eyes wild with passion as she swam in the sea of bliss.

Like a freight train barreling down the tracks, his speed increased as he neared his own release. With each plunge into her, Megan responded with an "oh" that rose an octave with every thrust. She arched her back, her hips thrusting boldly against him. Her body clamped around him seconds before she screamed out in pleasure. With a rough shout, he surged into her a final time, his climax pulsing within her.

He lay down beside her, pulling her leg around his hip to keep them joined for just a while longer. She leaned into him and shuddered, her breath coming in rough pants. He rubbed his hand over her smooth bottom, willing his own heart to stop racing.

"I missed you." She whispered the words, but they sounded thick and heavy.

"Does that count since I'm still inside you?" He kissed the top of her head as she gave a silent chuckle. She swiped at her face and her body shuddered, making him wonder if she'd started to cry. Megan wasn't one for tears or sweet talk, always being open and direct to the point of painful honesty. He didn't want to even ask if she were crying now, because being wrong would mean giving her bricks to build the wall between them he'd been working day and night to bring down.

Instead he held her close, breathing in her scent beneath the citrus of a new shampoo she must be using. He played with the strands of her hair until her entire body relaxed, leaning limp against his.

"Brandon?" Megan whispered, her voice thick with sleep. "Did you pass out first?"

"Not yet."

"Darn." She cuddled closer and he folded her into him, trying to remember the last time they'd cuddled. She wasn't one for snuggling either, but he liked this new vulnerability, this opportunity to take care of her rather than running parallel lives. This was the beginning of having everything he wanted.

Megan surfaced slowly, stretching her naked body along the softest sheets she could ever recall feeling. She'd never been able to appreciate the importance of thread count until she'd realized the difference between two hundred and twelve hundred was worth the price.

Memories of last night flooded through her, warming the

dull ache between her legs and spiraling heat through her body. She'd forgotten the soreness that used to follow a night in Brandon's bed, her body having accommodated to his size years ago. It was a pleasant tenderness, but one that made her glad to wake up alone and not from the gentle prodding that usually welcomed morning in his bed.

Her stomach rumbled, bringing her mind out of naughty dreamland and into present time. Today brought many messes for her clean up, and she wasn't sure where to begin. Brandon had called the coffee shop last night and said she wouldn't be in today, but she had to decide if she wanted to go back to working there or the bar, where she was going to live, how much she wanted to owe Brandon.

As she got up and started her morning bathroom routine, she wondered what Brandon wanted from her. Last night he'd seemed so completely the man she'd always thought he was that she'd made all kinds of excuses for his behavior of the last few months. It made no sense for him to be pursuing her when she had nothing to offer if he already had a mistress on deck.

She filled the Jacuzzi tub and tried to put it all together. She'd really only seen a kiss, and while she was not okay with him kissing Gemma Ryan, or anyone else for that matter, it very well may have ended there, in spite of how she'd watched them enter his penthouse together. She hadn't given him the benefit of the doubt, hadn't given him any chance to explain at all.

As she slipped into the water and turned on the jets, she knew she'd have to confront him sooner rather than later. She didn't want to drag things on if there was nowhere for them to go. And she desperately wanted him to have an answer for everything.

The water rushed around her and she hugged her knees to her chest, saying a silent prayer that she could have her life back. She wanted to feel safe and loved again, to have the shrouds of suspicion vanish and see things clearly. If only the niggling doubts would evaporate, she might be able to stand on her own two feet again without worry of being knocked back by yet another tidal wave.

She turned off the tub and drained it, wrapping a towel around herself as she opened drawers in the master bathroom. All of her things were there, in the same disarray she'd left them in. As she rubbed her favorite lily-scented lotion onto her body, her confidence grew that another woman hadn't made it into Brandon's bed. If he'd tried to replace her, surely these things would have been among the first to go as someone new cemented her place in his life.

She made her way to Brandon's dressing room where she'd always kept a robe, her lingerie and a few things to change into. The small section beside his shirts was painfully empty. She knew that the other closet was filled with her things, but it still sent anxiety through her to know she'd been moved out. She checked the drawers in the chests at the center of the room, somewhat relieved to find the bottom drawer that she'd stashed hose and jewelry in still held her things.

Maybe being apart had been as painful for him as for her, maybe he'd only moved the things he'd had to see every day. If only it had been so easy for her to remove his memory from her mind. Megan tightened the towel around her body and walked to the closed door leading to the living room. She paused with her hand on the doorknob, hearing voices on the other side.

She pressed her head to the cool wood of the door, but still couldn't make out anything but the rumbles of at least two different male voices. Adrenaline coursed through her at the thought of being caught in Brandon's penthouse in nothing but a towel. She'd be the talk of the town, but then she was already.

There was no telling how long Brandon planned on talking, especially if he was working. She wished she had the day to waste lying about his room, but there was too much to do. She might be tempted if he had a television or a phone, but he always kept his bedroom distraction free. There wasn't even an alarm clock on the bedside table.

She could stay trapped, or she could hold her head high and move forward. Her stomach fisted as she turned the knob and pulled open the door, every inclination of keeping her relationship with Brandon private warring with her current need to stop caring so much what other people thought of her. Despite years of effort, when it came down to it no one held her in the esteem she'd worked for, and so their opinions didn't matter as they once had. Her gaze snagged on the purple nightgown laying crumpled on the floor, but she didn't have the nerve to put it back on. She could go out there and stake her claim on Brandon in the nightgown, or she might be able to talk her way around to simply using his shower if she wore the towel.

With an arm tight around her chest, she walked purposely into the room.

Chapter Eight

Megan heard the low whistle before she saw Danny Reid turn his wheelchair to get a better look as she tried to slip into the spare bedroom with a minimum of fuss.

"How you doing, darlin'?" Danny had always looked at her like he knew her secrets, and given that he'd been Brandon's best friend for as long as she'd known him, she'd figured he actually might.

Brandon stared at her, everything about him seeming relaxed and yet curious. He probably wondered how she would play their first display as more than acquaintances. It actually gave her some relief to know it was Danny. She'd always found his mocking wit playfully refreshing, as well as his blatant honesty.

"Peachy, Danny. How's your morning?" She tacked on a smile as if she weren't standing in the middle of the room in only a towel.

"It's afternoon, sweetheart. You really need to convince this one you can get your own coffee so he doesn't drag my ass up here for meetings."

She blinked, her gaze searching out the grandfather clock by the entry. Damn. Two in the afternoon. So much for her day. She turned back to the men. "There's coffee?"

Brandon stood and crossed the room, pausing to kiss her

temple as he walked to the kitchen. "I'll get it. You get dressed."

"Not on my account," Danny said, leaning back in his wheelchair. "I rather enjoy the view."

Megan blushed, but gave a cute curtsey before rushing out of the room. Danny's warm laughter filled the room behind her and she started to think that maybe this would work.

She'd assumed everyone would accuse her of using Brandon for his money now that hers had evaporated, but Danny acted as if he were happy she and Brandon were together. Though of course, there was every possibility Danny hadn't been the least bit surprised to see her and knew what she and Brandon had started long ago.

She slipped into a teal blue sweater-dress that had been a little too clingy last winter. The knit of the material hugged her body, but not in the way that had once annoyed her. She ran her hands over her hips, wondering if Brandon had thought the weight loss was a turn on. She was finally as thin as she'd always wanted to be, but she couldn't keep it up long term. In fact, instead of feeling svelte and healthy like she'd imagined she would, she felt tired and weak.

Once her world stopped churning, she needed to get her health in order. She didn't want to see Briana until she felt better. She'd watched her sister battle anorexia all through their teens and knew the lectures that would come if anyone ever found out she'd gone days on only diet cola.

Tossing the unpleasant memory atop the pile of things she didn't want to think about, Megan grabbed a pair of knee-high black leather boots and carried them into the living room. She set them on the bench by the door where her handbag had ended up last night. The two men were still immersed in business, so she snagged the steaming mug of creamy coffee from the table and gave Brandon's shoulder a squeeze in thanks.

Their conversation stalled while she was in the room, but picked up again as soon as she entered Brandon's bedroom. It gave her pause, but she decided not to borrow trouble. She didn't care what business they were discussing. They'd already managed to take controlling interest in Carlton International and had begun to sell off the subsidiaries. It was only a matter of time until everything was parceled out and she didn't want to know the gory details.

She wanted to get Brandon alone so they could talk about what she'd seen, about what exactly they wanted to tell people about their relationship. She took her time styling her hair and for the first time in ages did her makeup so that she looked and felt like she used to.

Still, voices blended together in the other room. She didn't have any more time to wait. If Brandon had more business to take care of, they would just have to talk later.

When she entered the living room, all conversation stopped again. This time the air felt different, charged with something she didn't want to name. As she neared the table, both Brandon and Danny slid paperwork into folders and closed them.

"Don't hide everything on my account, unless of course, I'm why you're putting things away."

Brandon's smile was fake, his dark eyes fathomless as she came to stand beside where he sat. "Not at all, we're just finishing up for the day. Loverboy has a wedding to plan."

Danny shook his head. "I just have to fly to Vegas and have a good time. She takes care of all the details. You're both coming, right?"

Megan blinked, a little stunned that Danny had accepted her so readily, enough to invite her to his wedding.

"I wouldn't miss it. It's not every day you can marry off your two best friends in one shot." Brandon grinned, even his eyes smiling this time.

"Well, you did have something to do with that." Danny slid all of the folders into his briefcase and then snapped it closed before sliding it onto his lap.

"When are you getting married?" Megan's mind tried to figure out who he would be marrying. Brandon knew lots of people, but Danny was the only one she'd ever considered his best friend.

"New Years Eve." He looked to Brandon. "We should all fly out together. Maybe you can even talk her into inviting some of her other friends."

"Gemma doesn't want it to be an event, just a wedding." Brandon leaned back in his chair. "I know when my mom finds out she'll probably want to hold some kind of reception."

Megan's pulse thudded in her ears as things clicked into place. She scanned the room, finding her shoes and purse, but Cash's leash was gone from the table by the door. Brandon must have given him to the pet concierge of the hotel, a move that would send rumors through the hotel grapevine. Everyone would know that she'd been here, been with Brandon. But the waves of impending humiliation at being used and discarded were nothing compared to the tsunami of pain drowning her soul.

She looked at Danny's smiling face, hating what she'd just realized, hating that he too would soon be mired in the despair of betrayal. "You're going to marry Gemma Ryan?"

Danny nodded and raised his hands. "I know you two aren't the best of friends, but—"

"She's having an affair with Brandon." Megan stared at Danny, watching his eyes glaze over in shock. She didn't want to hurt him, but a clean break was better than the slow, strangling end she was experiencing.

"No way," Danny said, shaking his head.

"Megan, where the hell are you getting this?" Brandon had the decency to look confused.

"I saw you." Her hands shook as the memory replayed in her mind, an avalanche of misery hurtling towards her. Her throat tightened, but she continued, the words falling out of her mouth in a rush. "I came here for my birthday just like we had planned, hoping you could explain what was going on and figure out what to do next. Happy Birthday to me, I found you in the hall kissing her. I waited, Brandon, I waited for you to push her away, to tell her no, but all you did was open your door and let her in." She swiped her eyes with the back of her hand, wishing she were better at hiding her emotions.

"I can explain." Brandon stood and reached for her arm, but she shook him off.

"I'm sure you can explain it to me. You're good at spinning lies. When you bought my family's company without warning me, I got it loud and clear that business matters more than I do. But he's your best friend, Brandon. Doesn't that mean anything to you either?"

"Is it true?" Danny's dark tone turned both their heads.

Brandon pressed his lips into a line and shook his head. "Yes, but—"

"There's no but." Danny dismissed Brandon with a flick of his hand and started his chair towards the door. "I don't want your sloppy seconds. We've never double dipped before, and I'm not about to start now."

Brandon followed him to the door, blocking his way. "It's not like she said."

"Get out of my way. Don't be an ass."

Brandon stepped aside. "Fine, but you have to listen to me."

"Only for as long as the elevator takes." Danny wheeled through the door with Brandon two steps behind.

Before the door closed Brandon turned, pointing his finger at her. "You stay right there. You've got this wrong."

The door slammed and Megan shuddered. She wrapped her arms around herself and squeezed tight, wishing someone else could hold her. Pushing aside the pity and the panic, she grabbed her handbag and boots, sat down on the bench by the door and zipped them up.

The elevator for the penthouse was dedicated, but she could take the stairs one flight down and catch the regular elevator to the lobby. Still, she had to hurry because she doubted Danny was going to keep Brandon occupied for longer than the elevator ride.

It wasn't much of a plan, but she'd been living life one step at a time. Last night had simply been a short reprieve after a horribly dark moment. She'd known better than to believe it would last.

She made her way to the door and pulled it open, finding the only person she wanted to see less than Brandon.

His mother.

Brandon tore into his penthouse, yelling for Megan. His heart hammered so hard it threatened to leap from his chest. He charged from room to room, knowing he wouldn't find her but still needing to check. He let out a primal roar of frustration as he lifted her discarded nightgown from the floor.

Just like before, she'd vanished and left all her memories behind. Clothes on the floor, hairbrush on the counter, empty coffee mug on the nightstand, and her scent on his bed. This time he wondered not just if she was coming back, but if he wanted her to.

He'd nearly forgotten that afternoon when Gemma had told him about her stupid plan, too much had been going on with Megan for it to register. It explained her anger, the depths of her sense of betrayal, but nothing excused the way she threw it in Danny's face.

His Megan was kinder than that, and would have made sure she had her facts straight before sucker punching someone. This creature had no qualms about attempting to ruin someone else's life with conjecture and assumptions. And she should have known better. Should have known him better than that.

He pulled all the linens off the bed, having learned from experience that it was impossible to sleep in a bed that smelled like Megan without her in it. As he'd followed Danny, he'd known Megan would be gone when he returned. As much as he wanted to explain himself, it was probably for the best. If she were anyone else, he'd throttle her for hurting his friend.

Danny might want him to think marrying Gemma was a game, but Brandon knew there was more to it, on Danny's side at least. He should have mentioned the awkward kiss and even more awkward proposal, but it hadn't mattered enough to him to have it register. Danny was the only person he trusted not to take advantage of Gemma, as far too many people had, and so everything had seemed complete. But the devil was in the details, which was what made Danny so important to him in business. They complemented each other, and together had been able to accomplish in a few years what it had taken his father a lifetime to attain.

He didn't want to lose any part of Danny's trust, and

though by the time he drove away it seemed as if they were on even footing again. Shaky ground, yes, but they had enough of a foundation to build things back.

Megan was another story entirely. It cut him to the quick that she thought so little of him. She'd slapped Danny with what she'd seen, but he'd been stunned by it as well. It was a piece of the puzzle that helped others fit—why he'd become persona non grata with her, the motivation behind the hickey's she'd left him with a couple weeks back, and even the unmistakable distrust she held between them like a shield.

But understanding it in theory did nothing to help the rage burning within at being accused of something he would never do. If Megan was so certain that he would, that he had, she didn't know him half as well as he thought. Keeping their relationship a secret had kept it hot, kept it sacred, but maybe it had also kept them from actually knowing one another at all.

If Jordana Knight had been surprised to see her in Brandon's apartment, she took it in stride. As much as Megan wanted to get perspective and distance from Brandon and his web of lies, she didn't want to risk offending his mother.

For as long as she could remember, Megan had wanted to be Jordana Knight when she grew up. She didn't know the older woman well, which probably led to the allure, but she had an intelligence and quiet strength that everyone admired. While everyone dismissed her own mother as a party girl who married well, people respected Jordana and what she accomplished for the community. Someday, Megan hoped people thought of her accomplishments the same way, if there ever were any.

"Would you like to come in?" Megan couldn't help but feel awkward.

"No, I'm meeting someone downstairs. I just wanted to drop

off the pass card for the penthouse."

Megan blinked. "You have a key?" That no one else had access to the penthouse had been a condition of their relationship. Megan didn't want to risk popping in and finding someone else here.

Jordana motioned to the other penthouse. "Brandon thought we might like it, but I like my house. I'm finally finished renovating and I don't want to take on a redecorating project. Not with so much to do."

Megan took the card Jordana held out and slipped it into her purse, her heart rate climbing. She had nowhere else to go, and the apartment that had once belonged to her family might give her enough time to think through a proper solution.

"Since Brandon isn't here, why don't you keep me company downstairs for a bit?" She didn't wait for a response before turning towards the elevator and pressing the button.

Out of respect for the woman and self-preservation, Megan followed. If Brandon was in the elevator when it arrived, he would not make a scene in front of his mother. The empty car arrived and Megan breathed a sigh of relief as they stepped inside.

"I'm staying in the guestroom." She stared straight ahead, catching both her own and Jordana's reflections in the mirror. "There was a break-in at my apartment last night, so Brandon put me up for the night."

The older woman's perfectly arched brows knit together. "Megan, my son is thirty-one years old. I don't have any delusions about his virtue."

"Nor mine it seems." Megan stood taller, wishing people thought her more than a plaything. "I was just on my way to the police station to see if an officer would escort me to the apartment. They were processing it last night, so I didn't get to take much with me. Not that there is anything left." Her voice trailed off as her throat closed. She did her best to shutter her grief, but from the pity in the other woman's gaze she could tell she'd failed.

"Oh, honey." Her warm fingers curled around Megan's arm. "You don't want to wait for Brandon to go with you?"

She shook her head. "He doesn't want me to go back there, but it's my mess. I didn't make it, but I'm responsible for cleaning it up."

"That's the story of your life right now, isn't it?" The doors opened and Jordana released her hold. "Let's take my meeting quickly and then I'll go with you. You shouldn't have to do this alone. Any of it."

Megan followed her into the bar on the mezzanine level. They were seated so quickly Megan barely had time to wonder if Jordana would pull her support when she found out Brandon was no longer interested. There might not be much hope for the future of the Carlton Houses without Jordana's influence. It wasn't enough of a reason to stay with Brandon, but it would be something she'd regret.

"When was the last time you ate?"

Megan tacked on a smile and toyed with the silverware, trying to get it perfectly spaced. "I'm fine."

"You know, your mother always said you were the one she didn't have to worry about. But I see you struggling to hold it all together and I wonder if maybe she should have."

"My sisters kept her plenty busy." Megan's nerves calmed at the opportunity to bring the conversation back to neutral territory. "And so did looking after the Carlton Houses. It's amazing how much time it can take to steer things in the right direction."

A waitress stepped to the table and took Jordana's order for hot apple cider and cookies. Megan hoped the rumble from her stomach in response wasn't actually audible. When they were alone again, Jordana folded her hand in front of her on the table.

"How is your mother?"

"Fine, I hope." Adrenaline jolted through Megan's veins. Was this not a chance meeting, but a way to milk her for information? She met the older woman's gaze and saw nothing but sincerity.

"You haven't spoken to her?"

Megan shook her head and wetness filling her eyes until she closed them to stem the flow. "I hate this. You have been nothing but nice to me, and yet I'm wondering why you're being kind, why you're asking about my mother."

"She was my friend. We weren't terribly close, but I have been concerned about her." Megan felt Jordana's fingers wrap around her own and clenched her jaw.

"None of us have heard from either of them." She opened her eyes and sniffled, trying to regain her composure. "Every time I think I've had the worst day of my life, another pops up and takes its place."

"I know that feeling." She tilted her head, her platinum hair brushing her shoulder. The waitress returned and Jordana pulled her hand away to take her mug. Megan did the same, letting the spiced cider warm her from the inside out.

"If you hear anything from her," Jordana put her cup down, "I'd like to know that she's okay."

"So would I." Megan's cup rattled as she set it on the table, her head starting to throb as she wondered when that might be. She had a sneaking suspicion that Brandon's meeting with Danny this morning had something to do with finding the Carlton money. Danny had been a Special Forces operative and was key to the information gathering piece of Brandon's business. If he couldn't find the Carlton's, her chances were slim.

"Sorry I'm late." Gemma Ryan's voice trilled through the nearly empty bar. "There is so much planning to do, I don't know if I'll be able to pull it all together."

The leggy blonde swept in, kissing Jordana on the cheek and giving Megan an annoyed look. Something clicked in Megan, like sights focusing on a target. Most of her anger and frustrations didn't have a mark, but her jealousy had one very definitive point.

"Why are you in such a rush to get married?" Megan asked, her pulse racing. "Did you get knocked up?"

Gemma gasped. "I was talking about the Alzheimer's benefit. My marriage is none of your business."

Jordana blanched. "Girls, what is going on with you two? And Gemma, since when are you getting married?"

"Go on, Gemma. I'd love to hear how your stories match up." She stared at her, watching her chin start to tremble and getting no small satisfaction out of it when Gemma turned away.

"Danny and I are going to elope in Las Vegas next month."

"Elope?" Jordana asked. "What's the rush? You don't want to miss out on having a wedding."

"We want to be married, not engaged," Gemma replied.

"Are you sure?" Megan taunted. "He didn't seem so keen on the idea earlier."

Gemma's head jerked around. "What did you do?"

"Nothing I feel even remotely guilty for. Can you say the same thing?" She felt horrible for having to be the bearer of bad news to Danny, but not guilty. He needed to know his world had been turned around by his best friend and his fiancée. At least Brandon had betrayed her with someone she hardly knew. She glared at the bottle blonde, wishing she would disappear and stop hurting people with her selfishness.

"Me?" Gemma placed a hand on her chest. "You are a horrible person. I don't know why Brandon feels the need to help you, but you need to leave Daniel alone."

"I don't think that will be a problem for either of us. Knowing what I know, and knowing what you did, I think we're the last people he wants to see."

"I didn't do anything."

Megan shrugged. "Danny and I see it differently."

"I don't even know what you're talking about." Gemma's phone rang in her purse.

"Go on, you'll want to take that. Like I said, you'll want to get your stories straight."

"I think you lost your mind with your manners and your money." Gemma dug into her purse and came out with a rhinestone-studded phone. "It's Brandon. I'm going to tell him how obnoxious you are. Then he will stop feeling so sorry for you and you can disappear like your parents."

Megan only just managed to hold back the urge to hurtle her mug at the back of the twit's head as she retreated. She had to get out of this town because if she ever saw Brandon kissing that tramp again, she might wind up hurting them both.

Chapter Nine

"Mind telling me what that's about?" Jordana's dark eyes sparkled, her cheeks lifting in unexpected amusement.

"I really don't want to get into it." Megan reached for her purse and stood. "Thank you for everything, but I really should be going."

"Sit."

She responded automatically to the tone, finding herself back in the chair.

"Gemma is a nice girl."

"Gemma is a two-timing slut who got caught."

Jordana lifted one perfectly sculpted brow, as if showing off the cosmetic artistry were more important than Gemma's tawdry indiscretions. "If that's true, it's Danny's issue. I wasn't aware they were even seeing each other, but whatever happened, it doesn't concern you. Don't make her the target for your anger. You're better than that."

"You're right. I wish with everything in me that I didn't care. But even though I know what happens changes everything, I can't get it to change how I feel."

"And how is hurting Gemma going to help?"

"She had a hand in ruining my life, and I can't see her without wanting to throttle her."

"But she didn't have anything to do with the business deal."

"I don't care that Brandon took the company. I care that he didn't trust me enough to warn me a tsunami was about to hit my life and I might want to head to higher ground, but the business deal didn't do any damage I can't fix. He did."

"What do you mean?"

Megan closed her eyes for a moment, wishing she could confide everything and in return be given the power to make it all right again. But Jordana would make things right for Brandon, no one else. "You're his mother. It's your job to believe in him. I've seen some things that make it so I can't anymore."

"But what does Brandon's business decisions have to do with Gemma?"

Megan didn't know what to say, so she stared at Jordana, hoping the older woman could fill in the blanks without a play-by-play.

"You think that Brandon and Gemma..." Her voice trailed off and she gave a decided shake of her head. "They are like brother and sister. There must be an explanation for whatever you saw."

"I'm sure they're running through the options right now."

"It doesn't make any logical sense, Megan."

No, it didn't. Which made it hurt all the more. She couldn't find a place where she'd done anything to drive him away, having always worked to keep him so enthralled he wouldn't look elsewhere. But he had. "If I hadn't seen it for myself, I would have a hard time believing it too. In fact, it rendered me speechless, which is pretty hard to do."

"You have to think about this, it doesn't add up. Why would Brandon have called Gemma and me to help with the charity if not to help you? Why would he be taking care of you now?" She tilted her head to the side, concern shading her expression. "How does he explain all of it?"

"I know how it works, I've seen my father do the dance often enough. I don't really care to hear Brandon sing the same song."

"Don't you think you owe him a chance to explain?" Jordana placed her elbow on the table and rested her chin on her hand.

"I'm trying very hard not to owe him anything." Megan twisted her napkin in her lap.

"How long have you and Brandon been together?"

Megan looked up, startled by the question. "Why do you ask?"

"Come now, Megan. Let's not be coy. I know it's been longer than anyone imagines. I knew he was seeing someone, but he's always been private about that area of his life. It was almost five years ago that he asked me about cockapoo breeders. I didn't put any of it together until I saw you with the same dog I've seen at Brandon's penthouse on occasion."

Megan nodded. "Seven years."

Jordana's eyes darkened with worry. "How old were you?"

Megan felt her cheeks lift in smile at the older woman's genuine concern. "I was eighteen. Few people get to stay with their first love. We just blew up in spectacular fashion."

Jordana sat back in her chair. "I don't understand. You'll fight tooth and nail for a collection of women's shelters, but you'll hand the man you love to another woman without a struggle."

Her throat tightened and she swallowed over the truth. "I don't want a competition."

"Life is competition, Megan. You know that." She took a deep breath and leaned forward. "Do you think there is any chance, no matter how slim, there is an explanation for what you saw that you can live with?"

Megan moved her head from side to side, trying to shake reality into her brain. "We don't trust each other, and you really can't come back from that, no matter how bad you might want to."

"I disagree." She blinked slowly, her lips pressed together in the way Brandon did when he was thinking something over. "Did Brandon ever tell you why we sent him to military school?"

"He had a party on the yacht. He says it was almost worth it."

She rubbed her thumb against a perfectly French manicured nail. "I'd just finished radiation for my second round with breast cancer and we did a body scan and found it in my liver and bones. I focused on the next course of treatment and alternative therapies. I didn't think what fifteen years of my cancer treatments had done to Paul. I didn't think of him at all, and there was someone who let him forget everything for a drunken night."

Breath slowed in Megan's lungs, the world around her fading.

"I was hurting and scared and angry, and Brandon heard every ugly thing I threw at his father. They got in a fight that broke Paul's jaw and started a spiral for Brandon that wouldn't end. I was sick and he was angry at us both. Sending him away didn't fix everything. The first year we had to brace ourselves for when he'd come home on breaks.

"But eventually he learned how to rein in his emotions, probably a little too well. I got healthy and Paul and I worked through everything. It took time to heal for all of us, but I have a hard time thinking that Brandon would ever allow unfaithfulness to enter in to his definition of himself. So I think it's worth listening to his side of what you saw. And I'm not suggesting you forgive him or ever forget, but seven years is a long time to erase."

Megan nodded, both out of respect and because in her heart she knew she had to know what went wrong before she'd be able to truly move on. As much as she was tempted to run away and not deal with Brandon and his betrayal, that same behavior had kept her stuck in neutral for the last few months. She had to make a clean break.

The only way to do that was to ask the question she wasn't sure she wanted an answer to.

The door had barely clicked closed behind her when Megan was swarmed by the wagging tails and jumping feet of both Cash and Money. She knelt on the floor to greet both dogs, giving Money a good squeeze until she looked past the entry and breath froze in her lungs.

Gemma Ryan sat on the couch with Brandon crouched in front of her. Megan was glad for the boxer's height as her body sagged, her hopefulness evaporating. Her gaze caught Brandon's and the dark, foreboding look he gave her showed no promise of an explanation worth hearing.

She gathered up enough strength to put on a façade of anger to mask the devastating pain. She huffed her breath in disgust and rose to her feet. Her heels clicked on the hardwoods as she marched down the hallway to the guest bedroom, grateful that both dogs followed her. She needed them.

She wasn't sure what to do next but her pulse was racing too fast to lie down and sob like she wanted to. Packing a bag of clothes so she could leave was the logical step, but she stalled with her hand on the doorjamb of the walk-in closet.

Why was her first instinct to run? It hadn't kept her from being hurt. This time she'd be wondering when he'd find her, what it meant if he didn't try.

She pulled down a slouchy satchel from the shelf, deciding it would hold enough clothes to get her through until her next paycheck. Her favorite bag had gotten beat up from use, and then ruined during the break in. "Where the hell do you think you're going now?" Brandon growled from the doorway.

"The train wreck of my life boards in an hour. Can't be late." She pulled a blouse off a hanger and began to fold it.

"This is funny to you?"

Megan spun on her heel and faced him, wishing her heart didn't lurch. "I will not stay here and listen to your late-night routines with that slut." She tossed the top into the bag and grabbed a pair of flats.

Brandon snatched them from her hands and threw them at the wall, making both dogs yelp and retreat behind him. "You're not going anywhere until you've apologized to Gemma and Danny. You have no right to wreak havoc in their lives with your juvenile behavior. You have no idea what happened that day."

"Oh, my bad. I suppose I should have followed you in for a little voyeuristic action. You think I want to watch you go down on someone else?" She turned back to the clothes, hoping she made it before her face twisted in pain. He grabbed her arm and spun her around.

"Are you really this insecure?"

She wrenched free of his grasp and gave him a look that should have killed him on contact. Too bad it didn't even penetrate his hard veneer.

Megan was terrified, angry, hurting and beyond humiliated. A treacherous combination. "I guess we'll just have to wait and see how you feel when you see me face first in someone else."

"Don't taunt me, little girl." He stepped closer until she had to back up, the corners of the hangers pressing into her back. "You do not want someone else. You want me. And that's what has you rattled. You want to believe I did something reprehensible, because that keeps you safe."

"Funny, I haven't felt safe since you bankrupted my family." She sidled away from him and grabbed a pair of jeans.

"You're not going anywhere."

"I'm working at the bar tonight and I have a shift at the coffee shop in the morning."

"You're fired, and you're staying right here."

Megan turned slowly around. "Excuse me? You can't fire me, great and powerful Oz. You may have authority in the financial sector, but in the real world you're as much of a nothing as me."

"Ever wonder how you got your job back? Why the bar got a brand new security system?"

Megan felt as if every cell in her body were choking. Her pulse was racing, her head was reeling with conflicting thoughts and emotions, and the only thing she was sure of was that she needed to escape. "You can't keep me here."

"The hell I can't. You will stay put until you have calmed down and realize what a spoiled brat you're being."

"That's rich coming from you. Ever since you hunted me down, your behavior has been atrocious. This is crazy. You are stalking me. If you could channel this insane talent of yours, you could be a great asset to the country. Maybe if you get a hard-on for a terrorist, you might actually save lives instead of ruining them." She tried to get past him and out of the closet, but he grabbed her arm and pulled her to him.

"I am not stalking you," he said through clenched teeth.

"Get your hands off me." Megan shoved at his chest, but it might as well have been a brick wall. She couldn't move him, and touching him only reminded her of all the times he'd held her this tight. They'd played with dominance and submission, she'd tried everything in Cosmo to keep their sex life hot. Who knew the memory would activate now, when she couldn't afford to act on it.

"You're going to stay here and listen to what I have to say, and then you're going to apologize to both Danny and Gemma, and my mother for the scene you made today, and then you are going to do whatever it takes to make it up to me."

He lifted her off her feet and walked her back until she was against the wall. Though her mind knew it was wrong, her body reacted to him as it always had. In spite of herself, she felt the passion, the bloom of excitement swelling inside beginning to swirl with the anger drowning her. She knew it was wrong, and yet it was as if nothing could overwrite the programming of how she reacted to his nearness. She'd loved him her entire adult life, and nothing he did seemed to change it.

She had to get away, even now he was licking his lips and staring at her mouth. If he kissed her, she'd let him. It wouldn't be long before he was inside her and the lines she'd drawn would blur again.

She twisted in his grasp. "Let me go."

"Calm down." He held her steady, so she did the only thing she could think of. She kneed him in the groin and screamed.

Brandon's stomach churned as he dropped Megan to the floor and took a step back, just far enough so that she couldn't kick him. He crushed his teeth together and forced himself to breathe over the exploding ache.

Touching her had been his fatal error. No matter what she was doing, he could still look at her and see the woman he loved, no matter how deeply she was buried inside this cruel monster.

"Megan, are you all right?" Gemma's strained voice called out.

"Tell her you're fine," he ground out between clenched teeth.

"I'd rather tell her I'm leaving." Megan got up and tried to leave the walk-in closet. He held out his arm to block her path.

"Cash stays." It was mean and dirty, but it was the only card he had left to play. Not to mention he didn't want anything to happen to the dog.

Megan gasped and her blue eyes glittering as she stared up at him. "He's mine."

"Legally, he's mine. Purchased, licensed, registered, and you have no means to care for him. You abandoned him for months." He swallowed back the bile burning his throat. He'd destroy anyone who tried to take Money from him, so he knew the hell she must be going through.

"I hate you." Megan shoved against him, which made the residual ache in his groin worse. "Go, go be with your whore and leave me the hell alone!"

He took a step back, and Megan barreled out of the closet. She raced to Cash and scooped him up, Money hovering at her feet. If he didn't know better, he could swear both dogs were glaring at him.

He glanced at Gemma in the doorway, her eyes still red from crying and his ire reignited. "Stop embarrassing yourself by calling Gemma names. Megan, you're seeing everything through the lens of jealousy, and it's not very clear."

"Oh yes, it's all in my imagination. You would never do anything wrong." She knelt down, both dogs standing by her.

"I kissed him," Gemma admitted, her bottom lip trembling. "I'm sorry, it was stupid."

Megan was the picture of calm as she stroked the dogs. "Yeah, Danny seemed to think you're both rather worthless."

Gemma hiccupped. "You leave him alone. He didn't ask for this."

"And I did? Careful with this one, Gem." Megan tilted her head his way. "He'll take you for every dime just so he can try and turn you into some puppet."

"That's enough!" Brandon cut his hands through the air. "I've had all I'm going to take from your mouth."

"That's not what you said last night." She covered her mouth in mock embarrassment. "Oops, is she not supposed to know you've been playing with us both?"

"Brandon and I are not doing anything!" Gemma pulled in a ragged breath. "It was one stupid kiss, though if it keeps him away from you, it was worth it."

Brandon ushered Gemma out of the room and slammed the door, wishing that it locked. He wanted to keep Megan here until they both calmed down, but there was no telling when that would be. At this rate, they'd be in their seventies.

"I don't know what you see in her." Gemma collected her coat and he helped her into it. "You can do better."

"You don't have to flatter me." He smiled with a confidence he didn't feel. "You don't need a back-up plan. Danny will come around."

"He won't even take my calls. All he said was that he

wouldn't make it to dinner tonight, and probably not to the wedding, and then he hung up on me."

"I know." Brandon sighed, hating the aftershocks one moment had on so many lives. "Go to him. I'll admit, talking it out doesn't seem to be going well for me and Megan, but Danny will listen. He might not talk to you, but he'll listen."

Gemma nodded and then stretched up to kiss his cheek before thinking better of it. "I better not kiss you goodbye for a while. Your girlfriend might scratch my eyes out."

"That's probably a good idea. I keep trying to tell myself she's hurting, but I could shake her for what she said to Danny."

"You and me both." Gemma squared her shoulders and looked up at him. "He'll listen and he'll understand and it will be okay."

Brandon nodded. "You have an easier time of it than I do, trust me. Megan saw it, on her birthday, and when she was coming to have me explain what was going on with my takeover of Carlton International. It was a one, two, three punch. Anyone would have been knocked out by it. It doesn't excuse her behavior, but it does explain it."

"Kind of." Gemma gave him a sympathetic grin. "I still say you can do better."

After Brandon let her out he stared at the closed door, wanting to follow right behind his friend. He knew how to fix what was happening with Gemma and Danny. He didn't know how to repair the hole that had been torn in the middle of his relationship with Megan.

She was in the next room, and yet he missed her terribly. He missed her laugh, her wicked sense of humor, the way she looked at him as if he could slay dragons. It cut him to think he'd had a hand in changing her, played a part in making it so

151

that the things he loved most about her might never return.

He did everything he could to put off knocking on Megan's door. Phone calls, emails, ordering dinner, everything short of turning on the television and tuning out of his life. When room service arrived, he couldn't put it off anymore and knocked.

He wasn't surprised that she didn't answer him, but he was stunned to find the room empty. His heart ricocheted around his chest as he bolted for the balcony. His stomach lurched to find it empty. He looked over the edge, and then reminded himself that she was desperate and angry, not suicidal.

He paced the length of it as it wrapped around the penthouse, and wondered how she'd managed to get past him with two dogs. She was as resourceful as she was stubborn, which was how she'd survived these last few months. He climbed the stairs that led from the private balcony to the rooftop garden he shared with the other penthouse.

His pulse dipped from the danger zone when he spied Megan tossing a ball to Money, who scampered about the ridiculously small piece of grass while Cash had to sniff every single bush twice before doing his business. It was the same thing every time.

Heaven help the pup if another dog came along and changed the scent. They'd probably have to spend twice as long out here with him. That definitely put a tick in the column to join the penthouses into one apartment.

Brandon cleared his throat and Money brought him the well-loved tennis ball. He tossed it behind a potted palm. "Why do you have such an aversion to doing what I ask?"

Megan wrapped her arms around herself, her body-hugging sweater dress probably not doing much against the wind. "I'm not used to being told what to do. I haven't had a nanny since I was twelve, and I was the one calling the shots with her."

"Lucky you. My mother was still going to the movies with me at twelve." Money returned with the ball so he tossed it again, wondering when Cash would get around to deciding which bush got the honor today.

"You didn't have a nanny?"

He stared at the horizon, the lavender sky of early evening softening the edges of everything. "I was the only kid, and we had a housekeeper to stay with me when they were both out." His eyes met hers. "Did you like it?"

"Nannies? No, they annoyed me mostly. And usually wound up leaving suddenly because they slept with my father."

"I'm sorry." He looked away, wishing he hadn't brought up the subject.

"Don't be. It's just how men are."

He jerked his head towards her as if she'd slapped him. "Are you really going to put me in a box with your father?"

"Why? Don't you think both your egos will fit?" Money brought the ball to her this time.

"I am not like him, Meg, and in your heart you know that."

"I'm sure he used a line like that at least once. I'm sure over the years my mother heard every excuse you're going to try and feed me. She might have believed them at first, but after a while she'd lost so much of her self-worth that she just took it in stride." She turned and looked up at him. "Too bad my self-worth is all I have. I can't afford to buy any of your lies."

"So I shouldn't even bother with the truth, is that it?" Thankfully her dog finally decided on a bush.

Megan shrugged, staring out at the skyline as the day faded away. Her blonde hair danced on the wind and twice he had to stop himself for reaching for it to tuck behind her ear. When Cash scampered over to them, Brandon scooped him up and started for the stairs.

"I ordered dinner if you're interested." Money followed him down the stairs and into the penthouse. He fed the dogs, washed his hands and sat down to dinner alone. He was trying to decide if he had enough of an appetite to eat anything when Megan finally came in from the cold.

"I haven't had a meal in two days," she said as way of explanation. Brandon nodded, wondering if starvation was the only reason she'd deign to sit at the same table as him. She lifted the lids from each platter, and then switched them.

"Hey, you like the grilled veggie sandwich."

"No, I liked being able to fit into my jeans." She set his steak and roasted potatoes in front of her and began eating with gusto.

"For the record, you looked fantastic in jeans."

She pointed her fork at him. "You say that because you wanted them off."

He shrugged. "You look better with them off."

She gave him a pointed look that made him smile. Megan might be hurt and angry and lashing out at everyone she could, but she was still Megan.

Which meant he had to get her back.

He made his way to the kitchen and returned with a pint of spumoni ice cream. He was more of a rocky-road person, but he knew Megan couldn't resist the cherry-pistachio-chocolate combination. With as thin as she'd become, he figured he needed the edge.

He sat down across from her and carefully pulled his spoon through a swirl of green pistachio ice cream. She eyed him as he took a bite, her gaze narrowing when he lifted a spoonful of cherry to his lips.

"What's that?"

"You took my dinner. You can't have my dessert, unless you want to make a trade."

"I'm not having sex with you."

"Who asked you to? Your attitude today hasn't exactly been a turn-on." He tasted the chocolate this time. "I was thinking of something a little less unseemly."

"I'm not taking off my clothes either. You want that, you go track down your little tramp."

"Stop calling Gemma names. It's petty. And untrue."

"Hey, she's slept with half of Beverly Hills. You want to get in line for some of that, you go right on ahead."

Pain flickered behind her baby blue eyes. It was the only thing that kept him from walking out of the room. If she was hurting, then she cared.

"I don't understand why you didn't go with her. Unless you've tired of her already. Maybe she wasn't as good as you'd heard she'd be."

"I wonder if your nastiness is in direct proportion to how bad you hurt right now."

"Don't try and psychoanalyze me. I don't care what you do with your life, as long as you let me and my dog out of it."

"You wish you didn't care, Megan. If you didn't care then you couldn't hurt. But you do."

She rose from the table. "Like usual, you don't know what you're talking about."

He caught her wrist as she turned to go. "I'll make you a deal."

"Said the spider to the fly."

"Maybe." He grinned. "I want to tell you what happened. I

want to explain whether you care to hear it or not. You sit down and listen for as long as it takes you to finish the ice cream. Then you can go and lock yourself in the spare room, and I'll leave you alone for the rest of the night."

She shook off his hold and grabbed the ice cream. "Do your worst."

He waited until she'd settled herself on the leather couch before he sat on the upholstered ottoman opposite her. "I think I should start at the beginning."

"You mean you're not going to start with your tongue down Gemma Ryan's throat? And I thought this was going to be a naughty story."

"My tongue wasn't in any part of her."

"Oh, what a tangled web we weave..." Megan slid the spoon into her mouth, her eyes never leaving his.

Chapter Ten

Brandon stared at her like he had all the time in the world to convince her to believe his stories. His confidence mocked her and she tried to get her bearings. Hope bloomed in her chest that maybe, just maybe there was an explanation that could glue the shattered pieces of their lives back together.

Looking at him now, so close and so comforting, she wanted to believe he could fix this, fix them. His French blue dress shirt had long ago been open at the collar, but he slowly unbuttoned the cuffs and rolled them back to his elbows. His black slacks bunched around his narrow hips as he sat in front of her, staring at her as if sizing up an opponent.

His dark gaze held her in place, fixed on her as if he knew just how close she was to throwing in the towel. He seemed to see right through her bravado, like he could sense all her weaknesses and wouldn't stop until he'd exploited every single one.

Funny, how simply staring at someone's eyes could make your stomach pitch and roll, your heart skitter around your chest and make you doubt everything you'd built your anger upon.

"I think I've changed my mind." Megan silently praised herself that the panic didn't break her even tone.

"No, you're just realizing you're wrong about me." He

shrugged and spread his hands out. "You've been asking me for answers for weeks. I'm going to give them to you."

But he wasn't. He was trying to convince her to see things his way. Since it was far rosier than her version, she was tempted.

Being tempted around Brandon was a bad idea. She forced herself to think about her mother and wonder if this was why she never tried to break free. Had she let the shadow of doubt excuse obvious indiscretions? Megan couldn't let herself be fooled the same way.

He leaned forward, resting his forearms on his thighs. The scent of his cologne swirled around her, and she took in a deep breath on instinct, which only served to intoxicate her more. Why did he have to be so handsome and smell so good? It made keeping her perspective darned near impossible.

He gave her a slow smile that lit naughty lights in his eyes. He was so close that their knees were nearly touching. All he had to do was shift a certain way and that familiar spark would spiral through her body. She sat still in quiet anticipation, wondering how to keep her composure.

"I've been buying stock in Carlton International for years."

Megan blinked, her dirty mind getting whiplash from his businesslike words. "Why?"

"Because I figured your dad would divide everything equally when he retired. I wanted you to have the option of majority."

"But it's not as if..." She pulled her bottom lip between her teeth and tried to find the right words. She wanted to ask so many things, but didn't have the courage to say them outright. "Our relationship wasn't public knowledge, so why were you concerned about the future of my family's business? We were fun and clandestine. There wasn't a future for us, just a present."

"We were fun, but you're rewriting history if you think our relationship was some fly-by-night affair. No, we didn't share everything with the world, but we've been together for a very long time. We weren't talking marriage until last year, but we never once talked about ending things."

Megan leaned back onto the cushions, needing to get a little more space from the truth. She'd always tried not to think about the future of her relationship with Brandon. Things worked as they were, and she couldn't wrap her head around a life without him, so she'd always maintained the status quo. They'd outlasted all of her friends' relationships, but she always thought it was because the element of secrecy kept things hot between them.

"I collected the stock over the years, but a few months ago a large offering came out. I snagged it, and then started wondering why it was available in the first place. We investigated, and things at Carlton started to look shady. Some of the subsidiaries weren't doing well, but instead of consolidating, the company was looking to expand with an express hotel chain."

Megan pulled the spoon through the ice cream and lifted a scoop to her mouth. She let the flavors melt and blend, keeping her mouth full so she wouldn't be tempted to tell Brandon she didn't care one iota about why he took over Carlton International. She cared why he didn't tell her he was doing it.

"Since we had the stock, we could look at the financials. There was really only three days between when I was cautiously curious, until I knew he'd made some bad choices, and embezzlement was one of them. A lot of shareholders were involved, and I didn't alert you to my suspicions because I couldn't risk him being tipped off."

"You didn't trust me." A problem ice cream and excuses

couldn't fix, nothing could.

"He's your father." Brandon shrugged. "I would have protected mine."

She pointed the spoon at him, sugar-fueled confidence making her brave. "But if you were really as serious about a future with me as you are pretending to be, you would have trusted me with that decision rather than making it for me. You would have tried to protect *me* rather than your investment."

He winced and rubbed his hand along the dark stubble forming along his jaw. "I thought I had, Meg. I checked to make sure the trust funds were completely free of the business and they were. I had no way of knowing that he'd bled those dry too."

"And I didn't know to check because you never said a thing about it." She dug a pistachio from its ice-cream prison. "If you'd warned me I could have saved so many things, things they auctioned off that meant much more than money. If you would have trusted me, things would be different. You're asking me to trust you more than I trust myself, and yet you never offered me the same kind of respect."

"I know. I'm sorry." He placed his hand on her bare knee and a shock of something hot and reckless bolted through her.

He was firmly in the wrong here, and yet, strangely enough, it didn't diminish the attraction she felt when looking into his soulful brown gaze. He opened his mouth to speak again, but a rapid knock on the door stole their attention.

Brandon stood and pointed at her. "I'm putting both this conversation and your ice-cream eating on pause."

As he made his way to the entry Megan stared down at the softening spumoni and swirled her spoon through the colors. Growing up, her favorite Italian restaurant ended every meal with a dish of spumoni ice cream. It usually comforted her, brought back memories of her grandfather's fourth wife, Maria, who introduced them to the best bolognese in Beverly Hills. Maria had loved being a grandmother, and they'd all loved her for the five years she put up with Grandfather's penchant for the cleaning staff.

Megan took a bite, letting the chocolate and cherry melt against her tongue as she tried to make out the muffled conversation. She was four bites in before he returned with a plain white box.

"Do you ever listen?" He smiled down at her, the smile he used whenever she'd been waiting for him in nothing but his sheets after he'd worked late.

She shored up her defenses, determined not to fall victim to believing lies to better her life. "What's that? The ashes of another company you've raided?"

"I reallocate resources, Megan. I'm not some pirate." He lifted the lid off the box before carrying it to the ottoman and placing it beside him as he sat. "It's what was left from the apartment."

The ice cream curdled in her stomach and she set the carton on the end table. "What do you mean, what was left?"

"I had them save anything that wasn't damaged."

"The police?" Her hands were shaking so she folded them together in her lap.

"No, the cleaning service."

"You hired someone to clean up the mess?"

"I wasn't about to let you do it, and your esteemed property management company had a twenty-four-hour eviction notice on your apartment door this morning."

"They threw me out?" She blinked slowly, trying to wrap her head around why they would do such a thing. She'd been a model tenant. For them to toss her out on the street after she'd been victimized was beyond anything she could imagine. Her stomach churned and her eyes grew heavy as she registered another experience of how people preyed on the powerless.

"They're slum lords. Scruples aren't their thing." He reached into the box.

Megan tried to put aside her disappointment and despair and furrowed her brow, trying to connect the dots but coming up short. "How do you know what was on my door?"

She watched as Brandon's expression changed from cool confidence to indecision. She'd rarely seen him lose his sheen of certainty, and the change alarmed her.

"Did you have the apartment under surveillance?"

"Yes, but—"

"Let me guess, you can explain." She snatched the box away from him, troubled by how light it was.

"You weren't safe there. Obviously."

"So you had me watched?" She swallowed hard, afraid she might throw up. Maybe all this manipulation and emotional warfare was just a means to an end for him. Maybe she was just a pawn in a game he was playing, necessary for now, but easily cast aside once she'd served her purpose. "Do you actually care what happens to me or are you just looking for my father? Are you trying to use me as bait to lure him out?"

"You weren't under surveillance, just protection. They never stopped you from doing anything, but they would have stopped anyone else from hurting you."

Megan didn't fail to notice how he skirted her other two questions. He had the wrong daughter if he wanted to catch her father's attention.

"Are they watching me now?"

"No."

"Is that why you say I can't leave the hotel?"

"If you go, will you come back?"

She peered into the box, not able to answer his question. It depended on so many things, like how this conversation ended.

He pushed his hands through his hair, the tousled chaos achingly familiar to what it looked like after she'd been running her hands through it during sex. Which was not good. She needed to keep her anger burning higher than her attraction to him so she wouldn't be taken in by whatever excuse he had for making out with Gemma Ryan in the hallway.

"Do you understand that I didn't steal your family's business?"

She looked up at him. "Do *you* understand that your business dealings were not altogether altruistic? You want to play the Robin Hood here, and I'm the wrong audience."

"I wanted to help you."

"No, you wanted to play the hero and give me controlling interest the first time my sisters and I disagreed about something. But that wouldn't have happened. I don't want to run a hotel empire, Briana does. Ava and I would have supported whatever decisions she made because this is what she's studied, what she'd done internships to learn. If you would have asked me, I would have told you not to bother."

"Wow." He sat back, his shoulders drooping slightly.

"I don't care about making money the way you do. Until I didn't have any, I never really thought about money at all. I've cared about this." She pulled out her great-grandmother's Bible which she'd kept under the air mattress. She'd never been religious, but turning the thin pages and seeing the family tree written inside had calmed her. "My great-grandmother had nothing when she started taking in boarders so that she could keep her son fed."

"That's why I thought you would want the company, because of how proud you've always been of what she accomplished."

Megan shook her head and pulled another book from the box. "What she accomplished was having a very enterprising son who turned a collection of small hotels into a conglomerate. Have you ever read my grandfather's autobiography?"

Brandon took the paperback from her. "I can't say that I have."

"Neither had I. The book is in every nightstand of our hotels, right there with the Bible and the phone book. That copy is technically yours. I stole it from the Hollywood Carlton. I figured I knew him, so I knew the story. It turns out this—" Megan swirled her hand around the room, "—this was never part of my great-grandmother's dream. She just wanted to be an example of how a woman can be in a bad situation and make something good come of it. He was the one who wanted to live in Beverly Hills and have all the things he dreamed about as a child."

Brandon nodded, staring down at the book in his hands.

"If you had only invested in Carlton International for me, you would have told me from the start. You would have told me things looked shady. You would have told me to watch my back. Instead, I'm trying to stay upright in the middle of a hurricane and you'll barely admit it's raining. This wasn't for me, Brandon. This was for you to play a hero. I don't need you to save me. I can take care of myself. Maybe not to your standards, but I'll be okay." For the first time in a very long while, she knew she would be.

"You talk about yourself in the singular, as if you're alone in this world, and you're not. What you do affects me too."

"But I am single, Brandon."

"Like hell you are."

Megan closed her eyes and tried to draw on strength from somewhere, anywhere, because this was the part that mattered, the part that had her wondering if a soul could bleed to death.

Her eyes felt heavy and her throat ached. A part of her wanted to run far and fast before he said something that would send a pain so sharp and scything through her that she might never recover. She took a long, cool breath and opened her eyes.

"Seeing you with Gemma shattered every expectation I had of you." She swallowed over the lump in her throat, fighting to stay above the tears threatening to rain down. "I still have a hard time thinking that my Brand—" she brought her hand to her chest and fisted her sweater in her hand, "—the man I run to when everything comes undone, that he is you."

"I'm still me." He reached for her, but she jumped back as if his touch burned.

"I don't think so. But go ahead and explain to me how what I saw wasn't what it looked like. Tell me Gemma didn't really kiss you, that she didn't come here to have sex with you." She lifted her chin and prayed there was an answer she could live with.

"I can't."

His words hit her like a sucker punch to the gut. If she'd been standing, she would have fallen over. There had been a thin thread of doubt holding her up for all these months, and he'd just cut it, leaving her to tumble like a marionette without her strings.

Brandon cringed as her face fell. He wished he could rewind their lives and look up that day with Gemma and see Megan. If he would have explained right then, maybe she'd believe him.

"We're done here." Megan stood and smoothed her hands along the skirt of her dress. "Are you really going to try and keep my dog?"

"Yes."

"Then don't bring that whore back here again. The world would end up talking about all the things your crazy ex-girlfriend did to you both."

"I told you nothing happened." Her jealousy shouldn't be a turn-on. It was adolescent and crazy, but it also meant she wasn't as ready to write them off as over and done as she claimed.

"I watched something happen, so you need to change your tune."

"Megan, you know how I feel about you. What do you want me to say? It was an awkward kiss. There wasn't any passion behind it, so I didn't feel the need to be dramatic in telling her nothing would happen. We talked about it, she left, end of story."

"You're lying to my face." She shook her head slowly. "You know, your mother asked me today if there was any explanation you could give that I could live with. This isn't it."

"You told my mother? God, Megan, you're like a tiger caught in a trap, lashing out at everyone who gets close enough to help you. What am I supposed to say to her?"

"Maybe you'll trust her with the truth." Megan spun on her heel, and stalked to the spare room. Both dogs followed her inside.

Megan stepped back from the mirror and wished that she had sluttier clothes. She'd always veered towards tailored and classic because the cuts tended to hide figure flaws. Now that she needed a good hoochie dress, all she had were choices fit for charity functions, which was probably where she'd worn them last.

The strapless purple silk dress she wore had been sexier when she'd had more going on up top to fill it out. Still, the beaded band along her waist and the short bubble skirt were enough to catch a man's eye. If not, the stiletto sandals and bare legs would help.

Her heart twisted in her chest at what she was about to do, or at least make Brandon think she was about to do. She wasn't ready to start trying on other men, but she wanted him to feel how raw jealousy could rub, wanted to know if he'd even be jealous.

She tucked her phone and the key card to Brandon's penthouse in a sequined handbag and palmed the one she'd gotten from his mother this afternoon. There was no way she was going to simply allow herself to be trapped in Brandon's home. Her great-grandmother hadn't risen out of adversity by staying still. She'd tried everything she could think of to break free. And so would Megan, no matter how devious.

With her shoulders back and head held high, she stalked out of the spare room and straight to the front door. She didn't look for Brandon, but felt his stare heavy on her just the same.

"Where do you think you're going?" he bellowed, his steps torrential behind her.

She pulled open the door, not surprised when his hand reached in front of her to close it with a thud. She turned, wishing being this close to him didn't remind her of being in his arms. She lifted her chin and smiled sweetly.

"I need some fun."

"You can have fun right here." His gaze dripped down her body and she barely reined in the desire to shiver.

"I need more fun than you can provide. It might be hard to find a man who hasn't been with Gemma, but I'm up to the task."

"Don't say something you don't mean."

"Oh, I mean it. And after a few drinks I'm not going to care who I have fun with, provided I don't leave the hotel. That was your caveat, right? I won't be followed as long as I don't leave the premises?"

"You're not going anywhere." He stepped closer, until she was pressed against the door and had to tilt her head back to look up at him.

"What's the matter, Brandon? Don't you trust me? Oh, that's right, you never have. I'm going to go down to the nightclub, and I'm going to have a good time and I'm not going to think about how crazy you are being."

"If you want to go to the club, I'll take you."

"Why, do you want to watch?" She licked her lips and saw the sparks in his dark eyes, his nostrils flare in anger.

"Do you hear yourself, Megan?"

"Do you? You're holding me prisoner and using my dog as a hostage. You're having me followed and feeding me lie after lie. I don't want to be with you anymore. Get that through your head and let me go."

His hands wrapped around her arms and lifted her off her feet. His body pressed hers to the door, his thighs against hers keeping her from kicking him. A flash of heat swept up her body to rocket around her chest like a pinwheel in the middle of a windstorm.

She'd always found the way he took control sexy and edgy. It had fueled her fantasies for so long she barely had the ability to turn her head when he leaned in to kiss her.

Her skin was sizzling, her body was humming and try as she might to convince herself it was just a well-learned reaction, she wanted him. And he knew it.

Maybe he could hear her heartbeat or decode the short pants of her breath. Maybe he felt the heat radiating off her body or sensed the fire he kindled inside of her. He licked her neck from her shoulder to her chin and her body cried out for his touch.

"You want me," he rasped against her ear.

"Yes," she moaned before rising above the fog of lust. "I mean no. Not anymore."

His hand moved between them, up her bare thigh to cup her sex. "Are you sure?"

When his fingers slipped beneath the elastic of her panties, she gripped at his shoulders, but didn't stop him as his talented fingers touched her core. He knew exactly how she liked to be touched, exactly where to stroke and dip.

"It feels like you want me."

She hummed a response because words were failing her at the moment. She obviously wanted him, but she wanted more of him than he'd ever be willing to give.

"Megan." His hot breath tickled against her neck. "Say it, say you want me."

"I want—" was all she managed to get out before the hard, solid slide of his body plunged deep within her and stole her breath. She wrapped her legs around his back and her arms around his shoulders and hung on as he thrust pleasure upon her body. She'd expected a reaction from him, but not something so primal, so fierce it was all she could do to keep from crying out as he pistoned in and out of her.

She rolled her hips against him and found the right angle to launch into oblivion. Orgasm washed over her with splintering ferocity. She clawed at his skin, pushing her fingers beneath his shirt as the waves of sensation slammed against her, each one deeper than the last. She felt him shudder, the hard planes of the door pressing into her back as he leaned forward and spilled himself within her.

They both panted like marathon runners just past the finish line, trying to find some semblance of the control they'd both lost. Brandon found it first, closing his thumb and forefinger around her chin and tilting her face to look up at him. He opened his mouth to speak, but confusion washed over his features before he brought his lips to hers.

His kiss was a tangle of passion that went beyond lust, beyond desire, and was so potent that she was washed in the staggering awareness that this was exactly where she belonged.

An amazing elation followed by the cold hard truth of reality. Panic battled with desperation as she forced herself to break the kiss, to break the connection between them.

She pushed against him and he slipped out of her, letting her wobbly legs slide to the floor. She fixed her panties and her dress, not at all surprised by how little the previous moment showed on her. They'd found themselves in the same clench countless times. She tried to tell herself that's all this was, just a replay of an old bad habit.

She wiped her mouth and bent to grab her purse and the key card that had fallen from her hands and her notice. She used to love the way he could make reality fade, and now she feared she'd become addicted to his brand of drug. She stood and noticed that he too appeared as if nothing had happened.

"That was really stupid, Brandon."

"I think it's the smartest thing either of us have done all day."

"I'm not on the pill, you jackass. Or was that the point, were you trying the oldest trick in the book to tether me to you?"

She knew by the way he blanched it hadn't occurred to him. She took advantage of the shock on his face to open the door and make her escape.

Brandon shook his head to dispel the worry and grabbed his wallet and phone from the entry table. He pulled open the door, expecting to see Megan waiting for the elevator. No such luck.

He pressed the button, surprised when it opened instantly. She must have taken the stairs in an effort to avoid him, knowing he would follow. He checked the stairway, but hearing nothing he opted for the elevator.

He leaned back against the mirrored wall as the car descended three flights to the floor holding the hotel's restaurant and nightclub. The private elevator opened into the restaurant waiting area, still crowded with people waiting for a chance to get a table with views of Hollywood stars, or at least Hollywood from the windowed walls surrounding the restaurant.

He made his way to the pulsing bass beat of the nightclub, nodding absently at a few people who tried to wave him over. He was on a mission to find Megan and drag her back home before she found her way into some real trouble. He'd toss her over his shoulder if necessary.

His pulse raced as he scanned the bar and dance floor, unable to find her in the swarm of bodies. After forty-five minutes of searching, including a trip to both of the VIP lounges, he still couldn't find her. As he stalked back to the elevator, he called the security team that was supposed to be watching her.

"She hasn't left the building and her car is still secure in the garage," the bodyguard claimed.

But Brandon knew Megan was resourceful and had practically grown up in this hotel. If anyone knew how to escape unnoticed, it would be her.

There was no way to gauge how desperate she was. Would she go to one of her former friends who had been so cold to her last night? Did she have cab fare to make it to one of the Carlton Houses? Would she try and take the bus at this time of night?

Anger and panic and terror slammed against him, making his pulse pound in his brain. He'd been able to protect her last night, but what if she slipped into harm's way again? What if she did get pregnant and he never saw her again?

"Find Megan. Now."

Chapter Eleven

Megan ran her hand along the keys of the grand piano, but didn't dare press them. Her family's penthouse was a mirror image of Brandon's, the living rooms side-by-side, and she didn't want to take the chance that Brandon would realize the empty apartment next door wasn't so empty.

The top of the piano had been filled with family photos in gilded frames, but now everything was as stark as a hotel room should be, all personal touches removed and likely sold to the highest bidder.

Her father's high-tech entertainment system had been replaced by the hotel's standard issue models, the modern artwork that had graced the walls swapped for some truly ugly pieces that must have spent decades hiding in the basement. Just like everything else in her life, it was the same but completely different.

The master bedroom smelled like clean laundry, not her mother. The vintage shoe collection was gone from the room-size closet, as was any sign that someone had ever lived here. Her father's study had been replaced by the standard issue bedroom, just like at Brandon's. She climbed the stairs to the room she'd shared with her sisters with deliberate slowness. Brandon had his office upstairs, but here the Carlton sisters had taken over on the nights their parents couldn't be bothered to trek up the hill to the family estate.

The landing had once been home to a doll house and play kitchen, but those had long since been packed away, replaced by velvet chaise lounges and a bookshelf stocked with leather-bound classics no one ever read. Now the entire space lay empty.

She hoped someone would read those books.

Her hand shook as she turned the handle and opened the door to what had been her bedroom. Her heart sank to see the three twin beds gone, replaced by the same standard issue bedroom arrangement in any room in the hotel. It was what she expected, and yet it made her throat ache. She walked around the room, trying to remember it as it was, as she was.

A note on the closet door caught her eye. She read *personal property* and she furrowed her brow. She opened the door and found the walk-in closet just as crammed full as it had been since Ava discovered her love of handbags.

Three girls in one closet made for a tight squeeze no matter how rarely they'd stayed here, and it seemed even more had been added to the fray, including a cardboard box of pictures.

Megan sank to the floor with the box in her lap, thumbing through the photos that had been in frames throughout the penthouse. Memories of her first time on her pony, Ava's sweet sixteen party, sporting a one-piece while her mother and sisters rocked bikinis on the beach in Hawaii. It all flooded through her as fast as the tears spilled down her cheeks.

They'd had good times, happy family vacations and tender moments highlighted by the picture of her and Ava holding their newborn baby sister. It had been good and her father had thrown it away. He'd put a price on his children and tossed them to the wolves.

Megan could remember that he'd loved her mother once,

and over the years his distance from them all grew, other women on the fringe but always there. It got worse and worse until he destroyed an entire legacy.

Brandon would be the same way if she let him. She'd deluded herself for too long that he was different. The lies would get bigger, uglier, and eventually she'd be strangled by them just as her mother was.

She fingered a glamour shot of her mother, one that had sat on her father's desk right by the phone, and wondered why in the world she'd left with him.

"Well?" Brandon clasped the phone to his ear, his hand clenched around the back of his desk chair. He'd been pacing for two hours and hadn't heard a word from the high-priced security team Danny thought so highly of.

"We've reviewed the security cameras from all the exits, and we think she's still somewhere in the building."

"I told you hours ago that she practically grew up in the Beverly Carlton. If anyone knows how to come and go unnoticed, it's Megan." Realization clenched his jaw. He'd supported her in their game of secrecy, encouraged her to learn how to get away without being seen, and now she'd gotten away from him.

"We've also investigated other locations where we've seen her the last few months. It's our opinion she is in the hotel."

"Where?" Acid burned his stomach at the thought she'd followed through on her threat to find someone else's bed to sleep in, but the fire waned as quickly as it had built.

That wasn't Megan.

He put a hand over his thundering heart and calmed himself with the knowledge of who Megan was outside of her circumstances. She was a natural-born philanthropist, a nurturer at her core. As unexpected as their frantic lovemaking in the entryway had been, it settled everything.

Until Megan knew she wasn't pregnant, she would act as if she were. There would be a pass on coffee and wine, eating balanced meals, and she'd have a safe place to sleep each night. She would be Megan, his Megan, however infuriated with him.

"We will find her. We've done a sweep of the common and employee areas, and have started searching the unoccupied rooms from the lower levels on up. She hasn't made any phone calls and I was just getting ready to check her internet activity."

"I'm not sure if she knows how to use the internet on her phone. She usually checks her email from the computers at one of her shelters."

"She's online now."

Brandon shook his head. "I told you she left."

"Let's see, she's in her email program now. She's sent messages to both of her sisters. Nothing obvious there, but we'll analyze them later to see if they're cryptic."

"Wait, hold on. You've been reading her email?"

"We monitor all communications."

"Well, stop." His pulse raced faster than before, the need to protect her overriding his own need to find where she was. "I mean it. Back out of her email and do not look or listen to another of her private correspondence. Are we clear?"

"Sir, you hired us to find Mr. Carlton. Monitoring his daughters has been part of that from before we started guarding Megan. We need to act the moment they make contact with him."

"Megan is bouncing on rock bottom. She has no idea where her father is." He straightened up and looked out the floor to ceiling windows at the twinkling lights of Beverly Hills.

Megan was out there, somewhere, alone and running, and he'd been the one to send the wolves at her heels. No more.

"You've had three months to find Carlton, and stalking his very attractive daughters might get you hard, but it's not doing your job."

"They are the best lead we have."

"Then find another, or you'll be out of a client. Not just for the Carlton project, but everything. Danny may have faith in you, but I am rapidly losing mine. If I find out you've violated the privacy of any of those women, you'll find yourself as decimated as any of the companies you've watched me dismantle over the years. Are we clear?"

"Yes, sir."

"You've had three months to find an old man, and you've lost a young woman from under your nose. I'm not impressed." Brandon clicked off the phone and hurled it at the wall. The dogs' heads popped up as it bounced along the floor.

Brandon didn't want to face them, to tell two dogs he'd lost their mom because his head had been on crooked and he couldn't keep his pants on around her.

He bounded down the stairs, not at all surprised that neither dog followed. They were as disgusted with him as he was with himself.

How had he not realized how deeply he trusted her? He was completely confident in her ability to keep their child safe, and yet he'd worried about a business deal? About keeping an embarrassing secret for Gemma?

It was beyond ridiculous.

He stalked into the spare bedroom, looking around for some clue as to where she'd gone. Her half-packed bag still lay on the floor of the closet. She'd obviously had a plan, somewhere to run. Now he just had to figure out where.

The computer keys clicked beneath her fingers in the main room of the penthouse suite. It felt eerie to be here alone in the middle of the night, especially with everything stripped of the familiarity she'd known.

Still, correspondence and fundraising attempts for the shelters kept her mind occupied, so no matter how many times she had to look over her shoulder at the strangeness of it all, she kept at it. A Brandon-induced pity party didn't help anyone, but finding a solution to the pet problem with the shelters might. She'd sent queries to dozens of agencies in the last week, but now she had time to sort through the replies.

She was able to find possibilities near each of the homes. It amazed her that they'd never thought to do it before. She'd been so wrapped up in the idea that she was helping so many, she'd been ignorant of the women they hadn't been able to help.

Spending so much time in the homes lately had alerted her to other challenges, like young couples who needed a break, and mothers with teenaged sons who needed a place to stay with their older children.

She needed more houses, places designed for those who didn't fit neatly in a traditional women's shelter, but who needed help nonetheless. But since she was struggling to keep the doors open on the four she had, she didn't know where she'd find the resources to start three new homes. She just knew that she had to.

Her instant messenger chimed, a screen popping up in front of her. She saw her sister's handle and smiled.

"Late night?" Ava entered.

"I could say the same to you. Are you just getting in?"

Megan typed.

"It's six in the morning here. I'm starting my day."

Megan quirked a brow. "Since when do you get up at six?"

"Since I have a business to launch next week. No rest for the wicked."

Megan laughed, and then jumped as her vibrating phone danced across the desktop. She'd silenced it earlier when Brandon had started calling incessantly, afraid he might hear it ring and realize how close she was. She checked the caller-ID to make sure it wasn't him again before answering.

"Hey, sis," Ava said before Megan could so much as hello. "I got a ton of calls about you yesterday."

Megan walked deeper in to the penthouse and curled up on the stiff, patterned yellow camelback sofa which had obviously been designed for looking at and not sitting on. She pulled a tufted pillow onto her lap and sighed.

"People I haven't heard from in months wanted to know what was going on with you and Brandon Knight, and since the jerk hunted me down two weeks ago, I'm starting to wonder myself."

"When I figure it out, I'll let you know. In the meantime, I think I've hit the mother lode of handbags for you."

"Don't change the subject, though that was a nice try. You left a party last night with him."

"Yes, I did." Megan swallowed, wondering how much to tell. She didn't want to hear how stupid she'd been.

"And? Come on, this is me. I know you had a major crush on him when you were younger, and then we came back from Europe and poof, you didn't have the time of day for him or any other guy who looked your way. He's the only guy I can remember you chasing, and then when he steals Daddy's company all of the sudden he catches your eye again?"

"I caught him." In so many ways.

"Doing what?"

Where to even begin? "You said I chased him, and I'm saying I caught him. I held on to him until the day you and I fought at the hotel, my birthday. When I came to get an explanation about what was happening with the hotels, I caught him kissing Gemma Ryan." She choked on a sob and wished her sister were here instead of on the other side of the country.

Ava swore under her breath. "You're not kidding."

"I wish I was making up the last part." She wiped her eyes with the back of her hand.

"So, why were you with him last night?"

"It's complicated." She hadn't wanted to worry her sisters about where she was living or working, and they were both so caught up in fixing their own lives they hadn't asked. Megan hadn't even mentioned the financial concerns at the Carlton Houses. She'd always been as positive and upbeat as possible. And private. She much preferred to fix other people's problems than to share her own.

"Megan, after what he did to Dad—"

"He didn't do anything to Dad. Our darling father stole from us too. Let's not forget that." She blinked as she realized she'd just defended Brandon. Again.

"You don't know that. How do you know Brandon didn't take the money from our trust funds? He ruined Dad, that's why they had to leave the country."

Except Megan did know differently. She'd met with the financial advisors who managed the funds and knew her father had been the one to deplete them. But she didn't want to defend

Brandon any more than she wanted to villainize her father.

Megan rubbed her forehead with her fingers, exhaustion catching up with her. "Have you heard from them?"

"No, have you?"

"Not a word." She cleared her throat. "How did Mom seem to you the last time you saw her?"

"The same as always. I want to know why she went with him instead of staying with us. I've actually been thinking that maybe he told her it was a vacation, and then when they got to wherever, he told her they couldn't go back."

"But why wouldn't she call us? Do you think maybe something has happened to her?"

"Like what? A tragic manicure accident?" Ava laughed. "I think our lovely parentals are basking on a beach, waiting for it all to blow over, or for Dad to figure out a way to get out of whatever tangle he's gotten himself into. We'll probably hear from them on Christmas as if nothing has happened."

"I hope so," Megan said, knowing they wouldn't. "So you think they're someplace warm?"

"I don't have any idea. Is Brandon trying to get you to find them? Is that what's making things so complicated?"

"No, it's not that." Though she did want to find them before he had a chance to. "I want to join them."

"Me too! Work is hard." Papers rustled in the background. "Well, it's tedious. I'm up to my eyeballs in handbag rental legalities. It started to blur together last night, so I decided to get up early and tackle it when I'm fresh. But it's still blurry."

"Maybe you need glasses."

"No, I just need Jack to come home and look it over."

"So, you and Jack are..."

"Happy. We've been over this. Jack isn't like the other guys
181

I dated."

"But you said he liked to play mind games, and that's why you stopped seeing him."

"Really, it was that he didn't want to bend the rules for me. We're good now, really good. He's learning to be more flexible, I'm learning to stretch."

"You two sound like a workout routine."

"That's another story entirely. Tell me about this handbag mother lode you tried to distract me with earlier."

"Our closet at the penthouse is full. They didn't sell any of it."

"What about Mom's shoe collection?"

"Those are gone."

"Damn. Well, I'm going to have to hire you."

"Hire me?"

"Yes, I have employees now. Well, just the one until next week, but I do. I'll need you to take pictures of the handbags and email them to me with a cute description. I'll shoot you over an example. Easy peasy, and I'll have you make the initial shipments from there. Sound good?"

"Anything I can do to help."

When the electronic lock on the front door clicked, Brandon froze in place. His body locked tight in the push-up position as he stared up from the hardwood floor. Sweat dripped off his nose and the muscles along his taut abdomen shook with the strain at having been used to the extreme for the last two hours. Time slowed to the beat of his pulse, loud and heavy in his ears as he waited breathlessly for the handle to turn.

Megan inched open the door, a collection of handbags threaded on each arm. She stepped inside and kicked the door shut with the heel of her shoe.

Brandon's body sagged in relief for a moment before he propelled himself to standing.

"Where the hell have you been?" He wiped his slick brow with the back of his arm as he stalked towards her.

She barely had time to shoot him a haughty look before the dogs bounded down the stairs, their nails clicking along the marble floor of the entry. She knelt on the floor, greeting both animals with an affection he sorely missed.

She slipped Cash into one of the handbags, one so large he seemed to stand in it, and rose. Money followed her as she made her way towards the spare room.

"Aren't you going to answer me?"

"I don't have to," she said in a sing-song tone meant to drive him crazy. It worked.

"It is four in the morning, Megan. Do you have any idea what has been running through my head?"

She spun on her stiletto heel and lifted her chin at him. "More lies, perhaps? Is that why you've been working out? Trying to get more blood to your brain to help you solve the problem of spinning a tale I'll actually believe?"

"I haven't lied to you." But she was right on about the work out. A bout of intense exercise usually helped him solve any problem that came his way.

But this time there were no options.

"Right," she drew the word out. "Your definition of 'nothing happened' is just different than the one everyone else uses." She turned back around and stormed into the guest room.

He followed, not about to let her get the last word, especially if it was one against him. "You've got to let this thing with Gemma go."

"Wouldn't that be convenient for you?" She set the bag with Cash on the bed and slid the others to the floor. Money jumped back as the waterfall of purses tumbled to the ground. "We're going to have to agree to disagree on this one."

"No."

"You don't get a vote." She sat on the bed and Cash crawled out of the bag and over to her lap as she undid her strappy sandals.

Her bare legs were paler than he'd ever seen them, but they still held the sexy toned muscle and elegant curve of her calves that always distracted him. He'd love to spend an hour just running his hands up and down those legs. And after having her feet in heels that high, she'd do almost anything for a foot rub. It would be a great way to get her to sit down and listen for a change.

"Nice, Brandon." She tilted her head towards him as she rose from the bed and went into the closet.

He blinked and looked down, realizing he'd risen to the occasion as well. He grit his teeth against the physical reaction and stalked into the closet. "Would you just be reasonable? You have to stop running away like this. You could be pregnant."

She turned slowly, holding two tiny clutches in each hand. "I don't want you to think you can hold that over me as some way around your indiscretions. I am not pregnant."

"You don't know that."

"Yes, I do. I haven't had a period since this whole mess started. I'm not exactly the goddess of fertility right now."

He felt his eyes widen at the shock. His mind spun back a year and a half to the only other time she'd been late. They'd both sat outside the bathroom, holding hands and waiting for the longest three minutes of his life. He knew they'd both been disappointed at the negative result.

His entire perception of Megan and their future together had changed that day. It was in that moment that he went from sure to absolutely certain he wanted to marry Megan, to have her be the mother of his children. He hadn't wavered since.

The sweat still clinging to his body chilled his skin as he stared at her. "You're three months late? My God, Megan, have you taken a pregnancy test?"

She closed her eyes and rolled her lips in as she huffed a breath out her nose. When she looked up at him, fire lit her blue eyes. "Four, thank you very much. I'm not pregnant, just under a lot of stress, and not sleeping or eating enough."

"But now you could be."

"I'm not." She held his gaze with such determination it snuffed out the part of him that wanted to believe she was.

He held up his hands. "I give, Meg. I'm done."

"Hallelujah." She tossed the clutches out of the closet and grabbed more handbags from the shelf and did the same.

"What are you doing?"

"I thought you were done pestering me." She continued until she'd cleared off all three shelves.

"I'm done fighting with you. I've spent all night trying to think of a way out of this hole, and the only thing I can think of is to stop digging it."

She let out a bright peal of laughter before she swallowed her smile and gave him a serious look. "That is the smartest thing you've said in months. Now go take a shower and leave me alone."

"You should get some sleep instead of playing with purses."

"I'm organizing them."

"Yeah, it looks like it." He stepped out of the closet and had to duck to dodge a Berkin he knew had been meant for his head. "For what that bag cost, you shouldn't toss it."

"Crap, you bought that one." She snatched it off the floor and stuck it on the highest shelf she could reach. "That was the only one, right?"

"What *are* you doing?" He leaned on the doorjamb and peered into the closet once more.

"I'm working. Since you had me fired, twice, I had to find a new job."

"Purse throwing is lucrative?" She shot him a glare that should have made him turn tail and run, but he couldn't help the grin. This spitfire was his Megan, and God help him, he found her determination and tenacity as sexy as ever.

"Ava really believes this handbag rental company she's launching is going to hit big. But don't worry your pretty little head, there aren't any shares on the open market, so there's nothing for you to buy up." She emerged from the closet and placed her hands on her hips as she stared at the handbag mountain.

"So you're selling these to Ava?"

"No, just adding them to her collection." She wrinkled her brow like she was thinking hard about something. "I'm going to borrow your digital camera."

His eyes widened as she marched out of the room as if he wasn't even there. "Wait a minute."

He caught up to her and grabbed her arm, spinning her around to face him. "We've been up all night, and I am willing to table this so we can sleep on it. But if you're going to work, then we're going to talk."

"This is when I work, Brandon. My shift at the coffee shop starts at four in the morning. I am wide awake. If it bothers you, Cash and I can leave."

"Not a chance."

"Fine. You don't have anything to say I want to hear, so leave me alone."

"That's not happening either."

"Then you'll have to launch your diatribe while I'm working." She shook off his arm and climbed the stairs to his office with a determined sway to her hips.

He followed, more than happy to watch her climb the stairs. When they reached the top he held back, watching as she walked to the closet and opened it as if she knew everything inside. It seemed she did because she emerged with a pocket-sized camera moments later.

He cocked his head to the side and caught her gaze. "What are these pictures for?"

"The website." Megan tried to move past him, but he stayed in her way.

"Then you'll want a better camera, a tripod, and natural light if you're not going to do them in a studio. Which means you need to wait until the sun comes out and normal people are awake."

"I'll make do."

"Don't be stubborn for sport. This is Ava's chance. She needs every advantage she can get to make this work. Her website photos need to look as professional as possible, or this will flop, trust me."

"I don't trust you. You're just trying to stall me so you can brainwash me into becoming some Stepford girlfriend. No thank you."

"Megan, you know how many times I've been able to turn a company around with an image facelift. You can be as annoyed with me as you want, but my business instincts are spot on.

The other images for her website were done professionally, so yours need to be on par or she'll wind up having to redo them and you'll be wasting your time and effort."

She quirked a brow. "How do you know what her website looks like? It's just a coming soon page."

"I met with Jack when I was in New York."

Her eyes widened and blazed with fury. "Tell me you are not invested in Ava's business."

Chapter Twelve

Brandon's stomach muscles tensed as he fought the urge to tell Megan what he'd promised to say. It was a white lie that wasn't supposed to hurt anyone, but white lies had turned their entire lives into a gray area.

He rolled his shoulders and decided to trust Megan with Jack's secret. "I agreed to let Ava believe there were investors in her idea, and that I wanted to be one. She got to turn me down."

"What do you mean, you agreed?"

"Jack asked that I not tell Ava he's bankrolling her idea."

Megan gasped, her mouth dropping open.

"It's a good idea." He moved his hand to reach for her, but clenched his fist and opted to talk faster. "After what she's been through, he didn't want her to be open to failure. This way, if it doesn't work, she's not ruined financially."

"Just completely beholden to Jack Sullivan. No wonder you agreed to lie for him, you both think trapping a woman with money is the only way you can hold on to her." Megan tried to push past him, but he held his ground.

"Jack has complete faith in Ava. He's just trying to protect her. I get that."

"He's lying to her, making her think other people believed

in her idea enough to put up their own money."

"And it has bolstered her confidence, which is why you can't tell her right now. When the business is running smoothly, he'll tell her."

Her shoulders sagged. "I'm not going to go running to her, but that doesn't mean I agree with the tactic."

"Good." A breath of tension left his body. "As long as we're agreeing, let's talk about the real issue." He moved past her, walked to the far side of the office loft and pulled open the drapes to see the twinkling lights of the city below. The dark haze of evening still clung to the sky.

"If you've thought up another story about Gemma Ryan you want to run past me to see if I'll buy it, don't waste your breath. I'm broke Brandon. I'm not buying any of your lies." The tremor in her voice punched him in the gut.

He turned to face her. "You want a play-by-play of what happened with Gemma, fine. If you won't throw it in her face, I don't have a reason not to tell you."

Megan stepped to the sofa and began straightening the golden fringe of a tapestry pillow. "I don't want to keep rehashing this. I'm not going to change my mind. If nothing really did happen, it wouldn't have done nearly so much damage if you and Gemma had been honest with Danny from the beginning."

"There was nothing to tell, Megan." He fisted his hands to keep from screaming. "If you promise you're not going to use it to hurt Danny or Gemma, I will tell you every minute detail."

"Why? Are you afraid I'll compare stories and find they don't match?"

He ran his hands through his hair, resisting the urge to pull it out. "What is it you want to hear? I'm trying to do what you want, what you've asked for. And it's still not good enough."

"The only thing I want is for it to have never happened." Emotion made her voice heavy and thick.

"What you think happened didn't."

"If that were true, you wouldn't have tried to lie about it." She lifted her gaze to his and the pain he saw there seared through him.

"I am sorry it hurt you. But it wasn't the kind of kiss you think it was. She asked me to marry her, and—"

Megan swayed on her feet. "She proposed to you?"

"It was a business proposal. She needs to get married without a pre-nup or her grandfather's estate goes to some Antarctic exploration foundation." Megan stared blankly at him, so he chose his words carefully. "I told her we couldn't, that we were like brother and sister and she kissed me to prove me wrong. It was awkward and sad. There was nothing there to even warrant pushing her away. So I let her in and we talked over some options."

She plumped the pillow and set it back in place. "The best option you could come up with is pimping out your best friend?"

Brandon held up his hands. "She's trying to make sure the Alzheimer's center at the family compound that her father and grandmother are in is safe. When I told her I was marrying someone else, she had to find an alternative. I think Danny has a thing for her, so it could be good for them both."

"But you're not marrying anyone else. You can be her white knight. If you want to save someone, there's your damsel."

"You're being ridiculous."

"Am I? You want to slay dragons and she's the one in the tower, not me. I climbed down all by myself."

"There is nothing between me and Gemma. Never has been,

never will be. What do I have to say to make you believe that?"

"It's a matter of too little, too late, I guess."

"There is nothing I could have done differently. I've thought about this from every angle. You disappeared as soon as it happened. I didn't see you for months, and what happened with Gemma wasn't even registering in my mind anymore. It meant that little to me."

Megan shrugged, the bored look she'd perfected masking her features. "Can I go now?"

He couldn't contain the growl of frustration. "I don't know what to do or say anymore. We are completely deadlocked on this. What makes me so good at what I do is my ability to change perspective and see a way out of any situation. But with you, it's all too personal for me to look at objectively. I'm too in love with you to risk anything happening to you. So, no, you can't go. Anywhere."

Megan plopped onto the sofa, her eyes widening as she stared blankly across the room. "You don't love me. You love having sex with me."

"I have loved you from long before I wanted to, and will for as long as I'm breathing. And stop minimizing our relationship. I get that you want to make me feel as bad as you did that day, but you can stop now. I feel like I'm in the middle of a tornado, my feet aren't on the ground and there are things coming at me from all directions.

"I invested in Carlton International for you, bought out the company for you, and forgave you for abandoning me without a word the moment I saw you were safe. I've done everything to try and keep you happy and safe, and it was all wrong. I just want to get back to where we were, how we were. But I don't know how to get there while you're seeing everything through a haze of green."

Megan put her elbows on her knees and brought her head to her hands. Her forehead rested in her palms, so he couldn't see her expression. He watched her for a moment, raw and mesmerized.

"Say something," he whispered.

"I don't know if I actually believe you, or if I just want to," she replied without looking up.

His shoulders relaxed with the relief that for once, she'd listened long enough to hear what he had to say.

How many times had her mother bought the same lines? Had a similar speech propelled her mother to abandon her life and her children?

Megan wanted Brandon to be sincere more than she wanted her next breath, but she feared he'd just managed to find the right words to unlock her defenses once more.

Her mind warned her not to be stupid, but she was so confused. She didn't know if she'd be stupid to believe him after what she'd witnessed, or stupid not to after knowing him for so long. And loving him so desperately, she'd been willing to take only what he offered and ask for nothing more. She wasn't that carefree girl anymore, and she worried he'd be disappointed to find the complicated woman that had taken her place.

Megan pushed her fingers against her scalp, wanting there to be some way she could be sure either way. But she'd learned these last few months that there were no guarantees in life, no way of knowing if anything were as real as it felt.

She'd have to trust again at some point, but she didn't know if she wanted it to be now, to be Brandon. He had such power, not just over her financially, but the power to destroy her very soul by simply taking back those three words she'd waited years to hear him to say outside of the bedroom.

193

The couch dipped beside her as he sat and an ache rolled through her body. Instincts warred in her confused mind. One part of her was so delighted by his words she wanted to reach for him, to take comfort in his touch the way she had so often before. But another part of her was absolutely terrified that now, even making love with him would be dangerous.

He placed a hand on her knee and she drew in a shaky breath, willing away the tears prickling at her closed eyelids. Things were so much clearer when she could be angry at him, but now love and desire were washing away her anger, bringing her dangerously close to the shore she always washed up on when life got to be too much.

It was always Brandon she turned to, he was always where she ran. And yet, when she'd needed him most he hadn't been there for her. It was a lesson she'd learned, that she needed to depend more on herself and less on him. But was it a lesson that meant she could never again turn to him?

Was what he'd done a mistake she could live with, or was it something that would stay between them forever?

And would she even be sitting here considering it if he hadn't said "I love you".

Brandon cleared his throat. "Why don't we go take a bath? Maybe it will relax you enough to get some rest."

Megan pressed on her eyes to make sure no wetness betrayed her before looking over at Brandon. "Sex would only confuse me more, not less."

The muscles of his shoulders bunched as he shrugged. "We used to sit in the tub until the water was cold. I was thinking about that."

"We haven't done that in years." She wiped her fingers under her eyes, remembering that she'd put on makeup trying to make Brandon think she was going out. "Why don't we sleep on it. Separately."

"Megan, we can share a bed and not have sex."

She swallowed a sad laugh. "We never have before."

"Sure we have."

She stood and brushed her hands on the skirt of her dress. "Only if we'd already worn ourselves out somewhere else."

"That can't be true." From the puzzled look on his face she saw he really believed it.

"If you can give me one instance, I'll follow you right now." She met his gaze and held it, knowing the truth with full certainty.

His brows knit together as she watched him try to think of a solitary time they'd managed to keep their hands and bodies to themselves. His face fell and his eyes closed as he realized there weren't any.

He shook his head as he looked up at her. "I'm an asshole."

She couldn't help but smile. "To be fair, I just didn't show up if I wasn't interested. And there were times it was the reason why I showed up. I think sex calmed my insecurities about me, about us." His concerned expression showed she wasn't lightening the mood as much as she'd hoped. "Cheer up. It's not every day closet nymphomaniacs find each other."

"Megan, it's not funny."

"Okay." She drew out the word and twisted her hands in front of her. Brandon rose and wrapped her in his arms so quickly that she wouldn't even have had time to squirm away if she'd wanted to.

"I'm so sorry. I shouldn't have let it go on like it did. I just took what you offered and never stopped to think about why. I was immature and selfish and wrong. Just wrong. I should have stopped the game years ago. I just thought that if it isn't broke, don't fix it, but that's what broke us. It was my ideal situation and I never once stopped to think what it was doing to you. I took you for granted and I'll make it up to you. I swear."

Warning bells sounded in her head. He was saying everything, everything she'd ever wanted him to. And still she questioned why. She tried to break free of his hold, but he kept his arms around her. "You're getting me sweaty and it will ruin my dress."

"You didn't even remember you owned that dress two days ago."

She pushed firmly at his chest, and this time he let her step back. "Yeah, what's with that? Have you been collecting my clothes?"

He crossed his arms over his bare chest. "You leave your clothes on the floor, housekeeping has them cleaned, and my closet is full."

"My lingerie used to be in your closet. Was that the only thing you wanted me to wear?"

"This is where I'm supposed to say no, right?" His dark eyes twinkled as he grinned.

She returned his smile, relieved to have lifted the mood. "We agreed you were done lying to me, so best to play it straight. Besides, with as much money as you spend on lingerie, you either like it, or you wear it when I'm not around."

His laugh warmed her heart, but the way his stomach muscles rippled heated her body. Which was not a good idea because he would take any move in that direction as confirmation that she believed him and wanted to be with him, permanently.

"You should go to bed. I'm sure you have a busy day scheduled. I need to email Ava an inventory of the handbags, but I'll wait on the pictures for now. Can I use the computer up here?"

She watched him stiffen at the question and ice once again clogged her veins. She'd been right to hold back. He obviously still didn't trust her.

"What do you think I'm going to do, Brandon? Email my father from your computer? Call up dear old dad with some tidbit I lift off your hard drive?"

"That's not it, Meg." He looked like he had more to say, but she didn't care to hear it.

"In case you haven't noticed, my parents don't care what happens to any of their daughters. I know you can't wrap your head around that, but they stopped paying attention to what we did a long time ago. My family isn't like yours. There was never a whole lot of substance behind the public image. Neither of my parents have contacted any of us, and I doubt they will."

Fear niggled at her that she was speaking the truth. She could do without her father, but the idea of never hearing from her mother again made her jaw tremble, so she clenched her teeth together.

He reached for her and she recoiled, not wanting to get sucked into believing things would ever be normal between them again. She crossed to his desk and snatched a few sheets of paper from the printer. Intent on finding a pen, she tugged on the desk drawer only to find it locked. She cursed and looked up at him.

"Why do you even want me here if you feel the need to lock everything up? What was your plan when you leave for work? Do I get a babysitter to keep from stealing from you? I'm good enough to share your bed, but God forbid I might want some office supplies."

He cursed under his breath and clenched his jaw as he stalked towards her. Her shoulders tensed as he neared, but she didn't want to run. She'd suspected he was hiding the truth for months, and now that she'd caught him again, she didn't want to give him time to think up yet another alibi.

"Are you just saying what you think I want to hear? Trying to get me to trust you so that you can use me as some kind of bait to lure out my father? Well, you've got the wrong daughter for that. I doubt he'd cross the street for me."

Brandon reached out and wrapped his hands around her upper arms. Her whole body clenched as she closed her eyes and held her breath, sure he was going to shake her like a rag doll. He forced her down and plopped her into the leather executive chair that rolled backwards under the force. She gripped the arms of the chair as it knocked back into the wall.

"Not another word," Brandon said through clenched teeth. He fired up the computer and then lifted the keyboard, pulling off a key that had been taped there. He jammed the key into the lock, turned it and jerked the drawer open so fast the pens and pencils inside shook. He plucked out two small robin-egg blue boxes and slammed them onto the desktop before banging the drawer shut.

If she hadn't been holding her breath, she would have gasped at the sight. Instead, she made a choking sound and closed the mouth she hadn't realized had dropped open. Brandon cocked his hip against the desk and cut his gaze between her and the computer monitor and back again. The whir of the machine and the drumming of his fingers on the desktop sounded as loud to her ears as an airplane preparing for takeoff.

Her picture lit up the screen as the desktop loaded. It wasn't anything spectacular, just a snapshot of her eyes peeking out from behind the duvet of his bed. The day they'd had a little too much fun with the camera flashed in her mind and heat flickered throughout her body.

The confusion of the moment, of her life lately, crashed around her mind. Her fingernails dug into the arms of the chair, trying to find some way to center herself in the real world.

"You said you deleted those pictures. I watched you do it." Her pulse pounded in her ears, fear warring with excitement. They'd played with the camera, but it was never meant to be more than that, never supposed to be something either of them would look at later.

"Oh, for God's sake Megan." He grabbed the camera she'd taken from the closet off the desk and turned it on. Icons popped up on the computer, freckling her photo but not blocking it completely.

He held out the camera to her and she pulled back involuntarily. She didn't need pictures to remember what they'd done.

"Look for yourself. They're all gone except that one. Not everyone would recognize you with most of your face covered, so I saved it. I get to be reminded of us and you get to keep your privacy."

She didn't take the camera. "Other people have seen it?"

He shrugged and set the camera down. "Probably not. I rarely hold meetings up here. Still, sometimes it's called for and you never know who might walk behind you when you're working, so I figured it was safer than these." He leaned towards the computer and worked the mouse until a file popped up, displaying dozens of pictures of her.

Megan closed her eyes, not wanting to see her former life in thumbnail shots. Her mind spun faster than a tilt-a-whirl and she was struggling to tell reality from illusion. She wasn't strong enough to suffer another blow like she had on her birthday.

With her entire soul, she wanted to believe he wasn't

playing her for a fool, but the risk of being wrong would shatter her. It might not technically be a fatal wound, but with as tenuous as her grip on her old self was, it would kill the girl she used to be.

"There you go." The keyboard clicked under Brandon's fingers and she opened her eyes to see him staring down at her. He pursed his lips together and pushed a long breath through his nose. "If you don't want it, don't want me, you should go. You can take whatever you want, but do it quickly. I won't follow you. I'm all in, Meg. I don't have another hand to play."

He turned on his heel and bounded down the stairs, leaving her alone with two ring boxes and a computer folder with her name on it. She leaned closer to the monitor, reading the names of the files until they ricocheted around in her head.

Pictures.

Gift ideas.

Proposal.

Wedding.

Honeymoon.

Chapter Thirteen

Brandon braced his hands on the slick marble tile and hung his head, letting the spray of the showerheads pound his body. His throat ached, his eyes throbbed behind closed lids, and his chest was tight with anxiety.

He'd lied to her. Again.

He'd been so exposed, instinct had him trying to protect himself. He wouldn't want to follow her if she fled, but he wouldn't be able to let her go. He'd probably chase her for the rest of his miserable life. Nothing would ever be able to stop him, not even the embarrassing awareness that she knew exactly how much he wanted her, how much time and effort he'd spent planning a life with her. But of course, most of that had been done while he was oblivious to what an asshole he'd been to her for the last seven years.

Until a few hours ago, he'd always thought he was good to her. Now he saw that he was good to himself, never thinking Megan might need more than fidelity and generosity to be happy. He'd taken her at her word that she wanted a fun, private affair, and in so doing he'd taken advantage of her. If he really knew her as well as he thought, if he truly loved her unselfishly, he should have seen that she needed more a long time ago.

And now she wouldn't even let him make it up to her. He'd

hurt her so badly, so deeply that everything he did seemed to reopen the wound. He couldn't see a way out of the mess that he'd made of both their lives unless she was able to forgive him. It was the only way he'd ever be able to forgive himself.

The glass shower door clicked and adrenaline shot through his veins. He lifted his head to see Megan holding the door open, as bare to him as he was to her. Relief washed over him with the warm water and his heart went all hot and gooey like one of those molten chocolate cakes she liked so much.

He held her gaze for a long moment, time slowing as his world tilted back into place. Uncertainty twined with lust haunted the blue depths of her eyes. He took a step forward, reached for her and lifted her off her feet as he pulled her beneath the spray with him. She fit perfectly within his embrace, her arms wrapped around his waist, her head nestled against his heart.

"Brandon?" He barely heard her whisper over the sound of the shower. "I can't be wrong about this."

He threaded his fingers through her damp hair, tilting her head up to look at him. "You'll always be right by me."

Closing the distance between them, he brought his lips to hers and brushed a quiet seduction against her mouth. Her lips parted on a long, passionate sigh, welcoming him back home. He'd wanted the kiss to be tender and sweet, but before he could help himself he was sliding his tongue into her mouth and teasing her to join in the play.

He checked himself, pulling away slowly and smoothing his hands over her shoulders and down her arms. He twined her fingers in his and moved their hands between them. He brought her hand to his lips and pressed a quick kiss before he noticed her bare fingers. His stomach sank as he sought her gaze.

She must have recognized his searching expression

because she gave him a weak smile. "I didn't open anything. It looked like you had a plan and I didn't want to ruin that too."

His brows knit together. "You didn't even look at the ring?"

She shook her head. "I think I'd rather have the proposal."

His cheeks lifted in the biggest smile he'd had in months. "That's because you didn't see the ring."

"I haven't been waiting for something you picked out at a store. I only wanted to hear you say that you love me." Her breath caught and her eyes flooded, but she didn't look away, allowing him a glimpse at the depths of her vulnerability.

Megan, who hid so much from everyone, was letting him in. Just as he'd been the only one to ever share the beauty of her body, she was giving him entry to her soul as well. As amazed as he had been by the gift of her virginity all those years ago, he knew that this was far more intimate, far more delicate, and the only time she'd ever give anyone a chance.

He wanted to argue that he'd told her he loved her before, but he figured she'd call him on a technicality the way she had about asking her to marry him. They made love every chance they could, and so it would no longer surprise him if that were the only times she'd heard it.

"I love you, Megan." He framed her face in his hands and pressed his lips to hers.

About the Author

Jenna Bayley-Burke finds writing bio blurbs strange. Should she mention the blueberry-eyed kids or the high-school-sweetheart husband or the eight romance stories or the obsession with wine and chocolate? Should she brag on the workshops she gives for writers groups or mention her fondness for starting a new story (both reading and writing)? She's never sure when to stop, so best to leave it at that. If ever you're curious about Jenna, check out www.jennabayleyburke.com.

Accept no substitute...for love.

Take a Chance on Me
© *2010 Kate Davies*

The Lady Doth Protest Too Much

Jessica Martin is determined to earn a permanent teaching position at Summit High School. That means hard work, dedication, and even volunteering extra time to direct the school's Shakespeare play. Which leaves no room for romance—especially with a co-worker. She didn't factor in the school's sexy security officer and the delicious fantasies he inspires.

Too Much Of A Good Thing

Former cop Tom Cameron likes his job. Or he did, until the new substitute busted his orderly life right open. Now, he can't seem to avoid her—deserted hallways, empty theaters, classrooms after dark—but he's got too many skeletons in his closet to risk his heart again. Asking her out to distract her from the play's, well, *drama* is a friendly gesture. Nothing more.

The Course Of True Love Never Did Run Smooth

Their chemistry could melt down the science lab, and before long they're burning up the sheets off-campus. And uncovering raw emotions—a stark reminder that love isn't in their curricula. When a troubled student goes over the edge, though, the need to stop a tragedy brings them right back where they started—face to face with fat

Warning: This book contains sexy encounters in classrooms, inappropriate use of school facilities, backstage shenanigans, and illicit activities on a ferryboat.

Available now in ebook and print from Samhain Publishing.

He'll let her have control...until he's ready to make his move.

Pride and Passion
© *2010 Jenna Bayley-Burke*

The only things Lily Harris inherits after her father's untimely death are debt, scandal and loneliness. She doesn't protest when her father's business partner, Jake Tolliver, steps up to help with the mess she finds herself in—until Jake reveals the last promise he made to her father.

Jake may be as compelling to look at as a marble statue— and stir a frighteningly powerful desire within her—but no way will Lily agree to be his socially acceptable bride while he continues to bed his string of beautiful women—not without getting him to agree to a deal of her own first.

With a well-earned reputation as a feral hunter who goes after what he wants, Jake has his sights set on Lily, and her lack of options puts her right where he's wanted her from the first moment he laid eyes on her.

Jake's not above making Lily think she's having it her way if that's what it'll take to have his way in the end. But once he grows tired of playing beast to her beauty, he's not above changing the rules of the game until they're both playing for the same prize.

Warning: This title contains a hero used to getting what he wants, a heroine determined not to give in to him, some indecent proposals, a fair amount of pride, and enough passion to burn up everyone's control.

Available now in ebook and print from Samhain Publishing.

SAMHAIN
PUBLISHING

www.samhainpublishing.com

Green for the planet.
Great for your wallet.

It's all about the story...

Romance

HORROR

www.samhainpublishing.com

CPSIA information can be obtained at www.ICGtesting.com
Printed in the USA
LVOW040926130712

289846LV00004B/4/P